ALSo by
Tricia Rayburn

The Melting of Maggie Bean

Maggie Bean Stays Afloat

Maggie Bean in Love

Ruby's Slippers

TRICIA RAYBURN

ALADDIN MIX

NEW YORK   LONDON   TORONTO   SYDNEY

This book is a work of fiction. Any references to historical events,
real people, or real locales are used fictitiously. Other names, characters,
places, and incidents are the product of the author's imagination,
and any resemblance to actual events or locales or persons,
living or dead, is entirely coincidental.

ALADDIN M!X
Simon & Schuster Children's Publishing Division
1230 Avenue of the Americas, New York, NY 10020
First Aladdin M!X edition May 2010
Copyright © 2010 by Tricia Rayburn
All rights reserved, including the right of reproduction
in whole or in part in any form.
ALADDIN is a trademark of Simon & Schuster, Inc., and related logo
is a registered trademark of Simon & Schuster, Inc.
ALADDIN M!X and related logo are registered trademarks
of Simon & Schuster, Inc.
For information about special discounts for bulk purchases,
please contact Simon & Schuster Special Sales at 1-866-506-1949
or business@simonandschuster.com.
The Simon & Schuster Speakers Bureau can bring authors to your
live event. For more information or to book an event contact the
Simon & Schuster Speakers Bureau at 1-866-248-3049 or visit
our website at www.simonspeakers.com.
Designed by Mike Rosamilia
The text of this book was set in Cochin.
Manufactured in the United States of America
0610 OFF
2 4 6 8 10 9 7 5 3 1
Library of Congress Control Number 2010905111
ISBN 978-1-4169-8701-7
ISBN 978-1-4391-5592-9 (eBook)

For Lauren

1. I have two favorite parts in *The Wizard of Oz*. I know it's kind of impossible to have more than one favorite of anything, but I think sometimes, like in the case of the best movie ever made, it's okay to make an exception. Because *The Wizard of Oz* has *so many* great moments—like when Dorothy first opens the door of her tornado-tossed house to a bright and colorful new world. And when the merry munchkins and Glinda the Good Witch of the North welcome her over the rainbow and present her with sparkly ruby red slippers. And when she finally makes it to Oz with her new group of friends and they all get head-to-toe makeovers. With so many memorable parts to choose from, it's practically impossible to pick just one favorite. So, I have two.

The beginning. And the end.

It sounds weird, I know. My two favorite parts of the movie are the only parts in black and white. Most people can't wait for Dorothy to get whisked away from boring, gray Kansas and wake up surrounded by flowers and lollipops. Who wouldn't want to go to sleep and wake up somewhere over the rainbow?

Well, me, for one. The beginning and the end are my favorite parts because that's when Dorothy is surrounded by everyone who loves her most. That's when she's happiest. And that's *exactly* how I feel at home in Curly Creek . . . and how, after today, I might not ever feel again.

"Heads up!"

I duck. An overstuffed black garbage bag flies over my head and lands on the walkway in front of me.

Momma crosses the porch and squats next to me. "Is your room done?"

I lower my chin to my knees and frown at the sight of her fluffy pink bathrobe poking through the top of the bag. "Yes."

She rocks to one side, gently nudging me with her elbow. "Do we have any road trip snacks left?"

I lean forward and grab the open bag of potato chips from the step below mine. I take a handful and hold the bag toward her. "Are you sure you don't want any help?"

Momma takes the near-empty bag, then tilts it and pours the broken remains into her open mouth. "Yup. We have a very long drive ahead of us, and I need my navigator to be rested and relaxed."

She gives me the bag and stands. I stay where I am, on the top step of the dusty front stoop, as she selects a cardboard box from the lawn and carries it to the car. The rear of the tiny hatchback already sags from the weight of our belongings, and black trash bags stuffed with clothes puff out of the open back windows.

It's hard to believe how quickly the car filled up,

especially since we gave away a lot of stuff we didn't need. Mrs. Jenkins, Mom's boss at the Curly Creek Nail Boutique, got all of our pink dinner dishes, and Miss Amelia, my old babysitter and the lead day care provider at Curly Creek Li'l Peeps, got all of our towels and blankets. Some things Momma sold to Mr. Lou of Curly Creek Junk 'n' Treasures, like our TV and her self-powered treadmill. Thankfully, we didn't have to worry about packing up, giving away, or selling any furniture, since Momma had rented the house fully furnished.

But we still have to fit four boxes, three black garbage bags, two piles of coats, and one brown corduroy duffel bag filled with about a thousand balls of yarn and a dozen knitting needles into the car. All that stuff is strewn across the front lawn like a twister lifted our small blue house from its foundation, spun it around, turned it upside down, and shook out everything inside.

"Ruby Lee! Don't you dare leave me!"

I look up to see Gabby Kibben, my favorite person in the whole entire world (besides Momma), running toward me.

Like Glinda the Good Witch had for Dorothy, Gabby had shown up just when I needed her; on our first day of kindergarten, her momma followed her onto the school bus and handpicked me for Gabby to sit with. I guess I didn't look like the kind of person who'd demand the Fig Newtons from her lunch box or try to snatch the flower-shaped eraser from her pencil case. Anyway, for seven years we sat together on the bus, played together after school, and slept over at each other's houses on weekends. Now, I wonder for the millionth time how I'm going to survive without her.

"You can't go." She drops to her knees in front of me. "You just can't."

Afraid to speak because I know I'll cry, I concentrate on folding the empty potato-chip bag into a neat foil square.

"I mean, this year is junior high. *Junior high!* And in two years it's high school. *High school!*"

"And after high school it's college, marriage, kids, and the nursing home." I try to smile. "Do you really want to spend every second of every day for the next hundred years together?"

Her eyes widen. "Yes."

I sigh as my eyes fill with tears. "Me too."

She looks over her shoulder. I look past her to see Momma and Mrs. Kibben talking quietly near our car.

Gabby turns back to me. "Come on."

I shake my head as she jumps up and bounds down the porch steps. "We're leaving any minute. I should probably—"

"You should probably follow me." Reaching the ground, she runs to the side of the porch steps and smiles at me through the skinny wooden bars. "If you're leaving any minute, then we're down to seconds."

She has a point.

I tuck the foil square in the snack bag at my feet and hurry after her. As I run, I try to ignore everything I pass. Because if I think about the wooden cellar doors, where Gabby and I spent hours tanning every summer, or the yard's lone apple tree, from which Momma made the most amazing pies, or even the neatly coiled garden hose that always worked as a sprinkler on superhot days, I'll stop running. I'll lock myself in the cellar, climb out of reach in the apple tree, or tangle my arms and legs in the garden hose so that it's physically impossible to leave.

And according to Momma, we *have* to leave. Nana Dottie needs us.

"Stay right there!"

I skid to a stop, holding out my arms for balance and practically falling forward anyway. "What is that?"

Gabby stands in the middle of the backyard. She presses one finger to her lips, signaling me to be quiet, and carefully brings the big black box even closer to her face.

"Is it a time travel machine that'll take us back to last year?" I ask hopefully, trying to hold still.

"Close." Gabby presses one finger down on top of the box, and a flash of light brighter than the Kansas afternoon sun illuminates the backyard.

I close my eyes and cover my face with my hands. When the white spots bursting across the insides of my eyelids finally dim, I open one eye, then the other, and peer through my spread fingers. The light goes off again, this time only six inches from where I stand. I spin around. "Are you trying to blind me so I can't read the map?"

"Trust me," Gabby says. "That was a great shot."

"How can I trust you when I can't even *see* you?" I rub my eyes and slowly turn back. (Because, of course, I do trust her. Completely.)

"The flash always goes off, no matter how bright it is outside. And you have to keep the back taped so the film doesn't fall out. But besides those minor flaws, it's pretty much perfect."

I eye the ancient black contraption she holds toward me.

"I got a great deal on it," Gabby declares proudly. "But Mr. Lou said it's in excellent working condition and that the pictures look surprisingly professional."

I take the camera—and immediately almost drop it. "It weighs, like, a hundred pounds!"

"You'll never lose it."

I look up. "It's for me?"

She grins. "It's not quite a time travel machine . . . but I thought if we got a bunch of shots now, you could develop them later and have a little bit of Kansas with you in Florida."

Despite almost crying a few minutes before, I smile. "You know, there is one thing that would make all of this much, *much* easier."

"Don't." Gabby holds up one hand. "Don't even say it."

"One last little moment that will create one last unforgettable memory that I can hold on to all the way to Florida."

"My mom took away TV and phone privileges for an entire week the last time I got caught."

I pout. "Please?"

"And if I'm caught this time, I'll be serving my sentence alone." She gives me a look. "*All* alone."

I try to pretend like I don't hear that last part. "Pretty please? It's my very last best friend request—at least for now."

She pauses. "You're going to take a picture, aren't you?"

"No." I nod.

"One picture."

"A lifetime of gratitude." I cross my heart and manage not to laugh.

She takes a deep breath, exhales dramatically, and then sprints across the lawn. When she reaches the tall wooden fence that divides our backyard from Mr. Finkle's backyard, she grabs the tops of the wooden slates and hoists herself up. After making sure the coast is clear, she pulls up her feet and drops to the ground on the other side.

I hold my breath and raise the camera. The last time Gabby did this, Mr. Finkle spotted her from his kitchen window and stormed out to lecture her about the importance of respecting your neighbors—and not falling into their strawberry patches and crushing what could've been the annual Pick of the Year at the Curly Creek Summer Fair. He then came over and gave Momma the same lecture, Momma told Mrs. Kibben, and Mrs. Kibben took away Gabby's phone and TV privileges for a week.

When a few seconds pass and Gabby remains out of sight, I count to ten and lower the camera, ready to bolt across the yard and rescue her from strawberry-patch-protecting Mr. Finkle.

And then I see her. Launching into the sky like a kite caught in a gust of wind. I lift the camera and snap a picture right before she disappears again.

She reached Mr. Finkle's trampoline, safe and sound.

I take another picture, and another, and at least ten more after that—one shot for every time Gabby springs above the tall wooden fence. As usual, I can't help but laugh as she twists and turns her body into letters of the alphabet, performing a much longer, much more physically challenging version of "Y.M.C.A." Most people could never guess what she's spelling, since some letters look remarkably similar, like *D* and *E*, or *I* and *O*. But I know.

R and G. Friends forever!

I take one last picture after the exclamation point grand finale—when Gabby hoists herself back onto the fence, clearly exhausted but grinning from ear to ear. By the time she reaches me, we're both laughing so hard we fall to the ground, tears rolling down our cheeks.

"I'm *so* developing this film as soon as we get there." I flop on my back and rest the camera on my chest.

"You know," Gabby says, lying in the grass next to me, "Mr. Lou said some places will put the pictures on a CD for you."

"So then we can e-mail them?"

"It's almost as good as being there as things happen."

I turn my head to look at her. "I hate e-mail."

She turns her head to me and frowns. "Me too."

I stretch out my right arm, palm side up. Gabby's hand quickly finds mine, and we squeeze tightly.

"Time to hit the road, sweetie!"

I close my eyes at the sound of Momma's voice calling from the front yard.

"I can't believe you're really leaving me, Ruby Lee," Gabby whispers.

Since I've never had to leave anywhere before, I've never had to say good-bye to anyone before, and I don't really know how it works. But I'm pretty sure the longer

I stay here the worse I'll feel, so I jump to my feet and hold out one hand to help Gabby up. I throw my arms around her neck, hug her, and then somehow manage to make my feet move toward the front yard.

"There they are." Miss Amelia opens her arms wide.

"Aren't they just the sweetest?" Mrs. Jenkins tilts her head to one side.

"Town won't be the same without you two running around," Mr. Lou says.

One good-bye is hard enough, and I'm not prepared to say fifteen more to the neighbors crowded on our front lawn. I don't have any brothers or sisters, and neither does Momma, so these people, most of whom I've known as long as I've been breathing, are our family. They've been saying good-bye for weeks by helping us pack, bringing us dinner so we didn't have to worry about cooking, and throwing us a big good-bye barbecue on the town green. Just last night, they brought over pizza and root beer, and we all sat on the front porch, eating, talking, and laughing. (And crying, especially Momma and Mrs. Kibben.)

"Good news." Momma stands near the car, which is now completely filled, and holds up a stack of black cassettes. "Mix tapes. Courtesy of Mr. Lou."

"Great." I try to smile.

Apparently I'm not the only one in Curly Creek who's never really had to say good-bye before, because after this exchange, everyone just kind of stands there, staring and not saying anything, like at a museum. Or worse—at a funeral.

This makes me think of Nana Dottie, who recently lost Papa Harry. I'd never met Nana Dottie's second husband (Momma and I didn't even go down to Florida for his funeral), but she's apparently out-of-her-mind upset . . . because we're *really* going out of our way to make her feel better.

"You know, I hear there are a lot of knitting circles in Florida," Mrs. Kibben finally offers.

Momma claps her hands and bumps one hip against mine. That's the thing about friends who are family— they might not know exactly how to tell you good-bye, but they definitely know exactly how to make you smile.

Momma and I hug everyone one last time. When I get to Gabby, I hold on to her until fresh tears begin to brim, and then I make myself let go.

A singsong chorus of "Have a great trip," "We'll miss you," and "Come back soon," surrounds us as we get in the car. It stays with us as we pull out of the driveway and onto the street, and then it slowly fades as we start driving. I turn in my seat to watch everyone grow smaller through the back window, but Momma's records are piled to the roof and block my view. When I look in the side view mirror, all I can see is a black garbage bag ballooning from the back window.

And just like that, we're leaving Curly Creek, the only home we've ever known, for a faraway place called Coconut Grove.

Momma says I should try to think of moving as an exciting adventure. But what good is going somewhere over the rainbow if you have no way of knowing what on earth you'll do once you land?

2.

By the time we reach Nana Dottie's, I'm 100 percent sure of two things.

Five bags of potato chips in twenty-four hours is at least three too many.

And Florida is *hot*.

"I can't breathe."

"Have some water." Momma holds a half-empty bottle toward me.

"I can't drink." I slide down in the passenger seat. "No room."

"It's the humidity. You'll get used to it."

I turn my head toward the open window so she can't see me frown. How could anyone ever get used to such sweltering, suffocating conditions?

"Aren't the palm trees great."

I turn back. She's not really asking a question. "Momma."

"I mean, just *look* at them. They're so . . . tall."

"Don't you think Nana Dottie has seen us by now?"

"Sweetie, Nana Dottie wouldn't see a tornado unless it snatched her up and spun her around. And even then . . ." She shrugs.

I raise my eyebrows.

"What?" she asks innocently. "It's true."

"We've been sitting here for an hour. Nana Dottie's house is right across the street. If she hasn't seen us by now, the neighbors have—and they must be wondering what we're up to. Cops could be showing up, lights flashing and sirens wailing, any minute."

"I bet jail's air-conditioned," she says, as though that's enough to make me stop trying to convince her to get out of the car. Since it almost is, I sit up and reach for the passenger door handle.

"I'm going in."

"Don't." She grabs my hand. "Ruby, please try to understand. Nana Dottie and I don't get along like you and I do. She eats caviar and I eat Cheetos. She gets manicures and I give manicures. She vacations in Paris and I vacation in our backyard."

I've only met Nana Dottie twice, so the fact that she and Momma aren't close isn't exactly hard to comprehend. But, "We're here now," I remind her. "Like, for good. If you wanted to live in the car, we probably should've bought one with air-conditioning."

"How about we go in tomorrow? Today we can drive around, hit the beach, maybe check in to a cheap motel—"

"I'll bring you some ice-cold lemonade after I take an ice-cold shower." I lean across the gearshift and grab the keys from the ignition so she can't make a fast getaway.

"Okay, okay, okay." She holds up both hands, closes

her eyes, and inhales deeply. "I'm coming. Just give me one more minute."

I sit back and watch her breathe.

"Good," she finally says. She opens her eyes and turns to me. "I love you, Ruby Lee."

"Love you, too." I take my camera from my backpack, fling open the door, and slide out of the car. "Let's go."

Momma takes my sweaty palm in hers and we start across the street. Realizing I'm about to find out exactly what we left Curly Creek for, my heart suddenly feels like it's been snatched up by the kind of tornado Momma claims Nana Dottie wouldn't see coming. Maybe delaying the inevitable for another twenty-four hours wasn't such a bad idea.

"Have you ever seen such a thing?" Momma asks before I can suggest revisiting the option. "This is a *house*. For one person."

I raise the camera and snap three quick pictures. Houses are different in Coconut Grove. In fact, Nana Dottie's looks more like a palace. It's two stories tall, made of some kind of yellowish concrete, and has dozens of windows taller than Momma and I'd be if I stood on her shoulders. The front yard is enormous and filled with tall palm trees, shorter flowering trees, and colorful gardens that seem to stretch on for miles. Nearing the front door and peering through two sets of windows, I see a pool glittering in the backyard.

"I didn't know Nana Dottie was *this* rich," I whisper.

"That's why she left Curly Creek," Momma whispers back. "She wanted more than our little town could give her."

I look over my shoulder at our falling-down hatchback with its garbage bags for windows parked across the street, and then down at my jeans, T-shirt, and red Converse sneakers. Five minutes after leaving Curly Creek, I dropped an open can of Dr Pepper in my lap, and the spray dried an ugly brown on my jeans. And in Georgia, Momma hit the brakes to avoid hitting a cat, which made me lose my grip on the meatball sandwich we got for lunch. I tried fixing the damage with tissues and bottled water, but two round red spots still stained my T-shirt.

Maybe we should've stopped somewhere to freshen up. I know grandmothers are biologically programmed to love and accept their grandchildren no matter what, but it's been so long since I last saw Nana Dottie, this will be like meeting her for the first time. And judging by her house and the other huge citrus-colored estates in her neighborhood, it probably wouldn't have been a bad idea to brush my windblown hair and change into clean clothes to try to make a good impression.

But it's too late for that.

"Ready?" Momma gives me a nervous smile.

I nod, hoping I appear calmer than I feel.

"Now remember, Nana Dottie might be sad. Let's try to give her room to breathe and to not ask too many questions." Momma squeezes my hand, then gently lets go to reach for the doorbell. As I watch her pointer finger slowly get closer to the official start of our new life, I think, *This is it. This is* really *it.*

"The lettuce is limp."

Momma jumps and I stumble backward as the

front door flings open, unprompted. An older woman in lime green linen pants and a matching floral shirt stands just inside the entryway. Her hair is midnight black and puffed above her head in a perfect circle; her skin is orangey brown, like an old penny; and her lipstick is lollipop pink. She seems to be smiling at us, but her mouth is sort of frozen. And she sounded serious when she spoke—but not sad. More like . . . mad.

This woman can't be related to us. She has to be the maid or cook, since Nana Dottie is obviously rich enough to have one, the other, or both.

"Hi, Mom."

I try to keep my mouth from dropping open, I really do. My outfit isn't doing anything for me, so if I'm going to make a good impression, it'll be thanks to my ladylike charm and manners. And unfortunately, revealing my Slurpee-blue tongue to Nana Dottie before even shaking her hand doesn't exactly make me ready for afternoon tea.

But this is my grandma?

"You said you'd be here early this afternoon."

"It's three thirty," Momma says through her own frozen smile.

"Three thirty isn't early afternoon. Three thirty is midafternoon, teetering on the edge of late afternoon, which is practically evening. You might as well have said you were coming tomorrow."

"We hit some traffic," Momma says.

"Well, I made a delicious salad for lunch, and it's been sitting out for hours. I'm afraid it might be completely ruined."

"Thank you for the thought, but I don't think Ruby and I are very hungry anyway."

Then, as though noticing me for the first time, Nana Dottie turns to me, bends forward, and slaps her palms against the tops of her thighs. "Look at you! Little Ruby, all grown up. The last time I saw you, which was a very, *very* long time ago"—she pauses as her eyes dart to Momma—"you were about two feet shorter and running through a sprinkler in your underwear."

I try to laugh, but it sticks in my throat. My underwear has come up in under two minutes. That has to be some kind of record.

Nana Dottie stands up straight and brings her clasped hands to her chest. "You should probably come in and stop letting the air-conditioning out. Where's your car?"

I step aside as she comes between Momma and me and looks out the door.

"It's across the street," Momma says.

"Which street?" Nana Dottie steps onto the front porch and looks to the left, then to the right. "All I see is an oversized trash can on wheels."

"That's the one."

Nana Dottie turns to Momma, opens her mouth to say something, and then closes it.

"Should I move it?" Momma offers.

This sounds like a pretty easy question, but Nana Dottie inhales quickly and holds her breath, as though trying to pick an answer. "Yes," she finally says. "There's no street parking here."

Momma kisses the top of my head. "You stay inside and cool off. We'll be right back."

Through the most crystal clear, fingerprint-free window I've ever seen, I watch them walk down the front steps together. It isn't necessarily the fact that Nana Dottie doesn't *look* like my grandma that surprises me—it's that she doesn't really act the way I imagined she would. I mean, Momma's her *daughter*. And I'm her *granddaughter*. Even when family members haven't seen one another in a while, don't they still hug once they do?

I make a mental note to ask Momma about this later, then turn from the window and wander into the next room. I assume it's the living room, even though it looks nothing like our living room in Curly Creek, with its milk-crate coffee table, old TV, beanbag chairs, and random stacks of records. This living room has three couches, shiny wooden tables that hold weird sculptures and empty bowls, and a zebra-printed area rug that I really hope is fake. Instead of TV, there's a shiny white piano. The room's pretty, but it doesn't look like a place you could relax in after a hard day at school.

But the pool, which is visible through two sets of glass double doors on the other side of the living room, definitely does.

"Ruby."

I spin around to see Nana Dottie standing in the entryway. "Sorry." My Converse squeak across the living room's marble floor as I hurry toward her. "I didn't mean to —"

She holds up one bronze hand. "*You* have nothing to apologize for." Her frozen smile softens. "Now, I know your mother says you're not hungry, but I just can't believe that. What do you say we head to the kitchen and see about saving that salad?"

"Okay," I say, even though my meatball-and-potato-chip-filled stomach grumbles in protest, and I never, ever eat salad — ever.

"Ruby, how about we toss our stuff in our rooms, take quick showers, and then cruise through the neighborhood?" Momma comes in from the garage, her arms wrapped around a fat garbage bag of clothes. "Check out the sights, the hot spots, the local color?"

"We're having lunch now," Nana Dottie says. "We'll discuss our plans for the rest of the day when we're done."

I pause in the hallway, unsure if I should stick by Momma, who stands perfectly still with her mouth wide open, or listen to Nana Dottie. When Momma finally closes her mouth and shakes her head, I give her a hug and hurry down the hallway.

Fair or not, weird or not, we're not in Kansas anymore. And until someone gives me a pair of ruby red slippers, I have no choice but to tiptoe around in my dirty Converse and try not to make things even messier.

3. I think I'll start my own business."

"Oh?" Careful not to tangle the pink yarn wrapped around my hands, which I'm holding up and out like a football goalpost, I pick up my cheesy chicken burrito with one hand and take a big bite.

"Yes." Momma tugs on a loose strand, then winds her knitting needles around until it's neatly tucked and tied. "And I know what you're going to say."

"You do?" I ask around a mouthful of gooey cheddar.

"Yes. Like, we're in Florida, where, even in the dead of winter, people wear lycra instead of wool and sandals instead of socks. And where nights aren't any cooler than days, so people sleep under sheets instead of cozy blankets. And where people go so that they never have to bundle up in sweaters, hats, scarves, and mittens ever again."

I swallow. "I'm pretty logical."

"But you know what I say?"

"Sweating's good for the skin?"

She stops twirling the knitting needles long enough to glance around and make sure no one's listening. "Two words." She leans toward me. "Senior. Citizens."

"Huh."

"They're always cold." She lowers her sunglasses and winks, then opens her mouth and nods to my plate.

I pick up the burrito and hold it out for her to take a bite.

"Just you wait." She knits as she chews, the flying needles glinting in the afternoon sun. "Total jackpot."

"Momma," I say, not wanting to steer her away

from her favorite topic but also knowing that we might sit here for hours if I don't, "I think I'm ready to go in now."

Her needles freeze. "Are you sure? Because we're in no rush. We can take as long as you want."

Unfortunately, we don't have that kind of time. We've already put it off for an entire week, choosing to swim and sun instead. "School starts in five days. We should probably just get it over with."

She narrows her eyes, apparently trying to judge whether I'm really sure. "Okay," she says a second later. "Junior high, here you come."

Junior high. I knew leaving elementary school forever would feel kind of strange—it was the only school I ever attended. Plus some pretty major things, like changing classes and going to boy-girl birthday parties, are supposed to start once you hit seventh grade. But leaving elementary school for Sweet Citrus Junior High is like leaving my life for someone else's. Not helping is the fact that my new school looks nothing like my old one. In fact, it looks like a bigger version of Nana Dottie's house. It even has its own outdoor Mexican restaurant, which, coincidentally, has a great view of the Atlantic Ocean across the street.

"After this, the day's yours," Momma says as we head for the front doors. "We can do whatever you want, wherever you want. Beach, movies, Disney World, you name it."

I try to smile. It's a nice offer, but it's not like we can ride Space Mountain after school every day. Or that those three exciting minutes will make up for the seven hours that come before.

"Name."

Momma and I stop short just inside the building.

"Name, please," the deep voice says again.

We spin around. A tired-looking man peers at us from behind a glass partition.

"Francine Lee." Momma strides toward the window like she knew it was there all along. "And this is my daughter, Ruby."

"Pleasure," the man says. "I'm George Fox. Do you have an appointment?"

"We're here to sign up for school," Momma says. "We just moved from Kansas."

"So you don't have an appointment."

Momma looks down at me, then back at him. "Well, no. I didn't know —"

"I've got a code green in quadrant 1A," Mr. Fox says to no one in particular.

I peer through the glass and into some sort of control room. There's a long electronic board with blinking lights and five small television screens that flash shots of empty hallways, classrooms, and courtyards.

"Will conduct a thorough search, then permit them to enter. Ten-four, out."

"All I want to do is sign my daughter up for school," Momma tries again, her eyes following his movements. "I apologize for not making an appointment. Should we come back later?"

"That won't be necessary." Mr. Fox comes out from the control room holding a long, thin, metal device.

"Neither will *that*." Momma grabs my hand and pulls me back toward the door.

He stops where he is and holds up the pole for inspection. "It's a metal detector. The door units won't be up and running till the kids return next week."

I glance behind us. The inside of each doorway is framed by a large gray box.

"I just have to give you a quick once-over with the wand. Like when you go through airport security. Standard procedure."

This is mildly comforting—I've never been on a plane before, but I've seen enough movies to get the idea. Still, I'm not at the airport; I'm at *school*. What's with the high security?

Noticing my concern, Mr. Fox adds, "Don't worry. Sweet Citrus Junior High is about as pleasant as its name. But all the schools have them, and you can never be too careful."

"Not all schools have them," I say.

"My apologies, Miss Ruby," he says, looking amused. "But you're not in—"

"Kansas anymore," I finish glumly. "Yes, I know."

Momma holds on to my hand as he steps toward

us and demonstrates the metal detector by waving it in front of his chest. He turns to me, and I close my eyes as he quickly lifts and lowers the wand over my clothes. I must pass the test, because by the time I open my eyes ten seconds later, he's moved on to Momma.

Anxious to get going, I take two steps down the hall. But then the metal detector starts whining—soft and slowly at first, then louder and faster.

Mr. Fox holds the wand above Momma's pocketbook. "Cell phone? iPod? BlackBerry? Common culprits, every one."

"I don't have any of those things." Momma's cheeks redden as she reaches into her pocketbook and pulls out her knitting needles.

"Momma holds the Kansas state record for purling," I explain when Mr. Fox looks surprised. "May we please go now?"

"Of course." He steps aside and raises the metal detector wand in mock salute. "Welcome to Sweet Citrus Junior High."

"Sweetie, I know what you're going to say," Momma

says as we walk down the hall. "But I promise this is a great school. Nana Dottie has extremely high educational standards, and she never would've given the green light if she thought it was going to be anything but the best for you."

Well, *that* is hard to believe. Nana Dottie hardly knows me, and she hasn't tried very hard to *get* to know me. The only thing she asked me in the past week was whether I liked my tofu grilled or baked. When I told her I'd never had tofu, she simply made it the way she liked it: grilled, sprinkled with lemon, and served on a mountain of lettuce. So while I appreciate the thought, I don't really buy it.

Just as I'm about to remind Momma of the tofu incident, she puts her arm around my shoulders and steers me toward the main office.

"You didn't make an appointment?"

Momma's smile fades when the woman behind the counter clucks her tongue.

"I'm Ruby Lee, and this is my momma, Francine Lee. We've just come here from Kansas, and we'd like to sign me up for school." I ignore Momma's surprised look. I don't want to be there any longer than necessary. "Please."

"Ruby's a very good student. I have all of her records here." Momma pulls a manila folder from her purse.

The woman's chewing a big wad of green bubble gum, and she snaps it three times as she seems to consider us. "Fill this out," she finally says, sliding a packet of papers across the counter.

We sit on a bench near the office door, and while Momma concentrates on the paperwork, I look around. The woman behind the counter is now sitting behind a desk; her orange-blond hair sticks out above the top of the computer screen, and her nails tap loudly against the keyboard. Two other women sit at nearby desks, also tapping away. They all wear an assortment of neon-colored capri pants, miniskirts, sleeveless shirts, and high-heeled sandals. And they are all very, very tan.

I'm wearing the same jeans I wore on the drive down (though they've been washed), a black T-shirt, and my

Converse without socks. Momma's wearing navy blue shorts, a white T-shirt, and brown canvas flip-flops. And while we've spent more time in the sun this week than we have every summer before now put together, we lathered on SPF 50 and still look ghostly pale compared to these ladies.

"Lois, I really don't have time for this."

I lean against Momma as the office door swings open and almost hits me in the head.

"I have tennis in twenty minutes, a kayaking date with Trevor an hour after that, and the most important shopping event of the entire year at the Lemon Grove Mall with Megan, Stephanie, and Hilary after that."

The tall girl with long white-blond hair doesn't bother holding the door open for the short brunette who follows close behind, shuffling papers and looking frazzled.

"Ava Grand." The woman who frowned at Momma and me when we came in now jumps up, all smiles and arms outstretched. "So good to see you, sweetie! You look fabulous."

"Thanks, Marie."

I glance at Momma. Do all kids call adults by their first names in Florida?

And do they all dress like *that*? Ava's wearing a short white skirt, a fitted light blue tank top, and wedge sandals with three-inch heels. My idea of accessorizing is wearing a rubber band on my wrist in case I want to tie my hair up, but Ava's idea includes a white leather purse three times the size of my old purple backpack and a shiny pink watch with a face so big it could probably work as a clock if you hung it on the wall.

She's definitely a few years older than I am, maybe even in high school, but she still looks young enough to call "Marie" Ms. Mean Office Lady (or Smith, or Jones, or whatever).

"I have a huge problem," Ava says sweetly.

"We're here to help," Marie promises.

"My parents made it very clear months ago that I absolutely had to have English with Tom Crane, and that math with Elizabeth Brinkley was absolutely unacceptable." Ava holds out one hand, into which Lois places a single sheet of paper. "So you can imagine my surprise when my schedule came in the mail completely incorrect."

Marie takes the paper and examines it closely.

"I mean, it's like it went to the wrong address or something." Ava laughs, as though generously willing to forgive the mishap once corrected.

"My apologies, Ava. Let me see what I can do."

As Marie scurries to her desk, Ava turns away from the counter. I look down at the papers on Momma's lap, but not fast enough.

"Are you new?"

I raise my eyes to make sure she's talking to me, then nod.

"Cool. Where are you from?"

"Kansas."

"Is that near Naples?" She tilts her head and squints, as though trying to mentally place it on a Florida map.

"Honey, I found the problem." Marie returns to the counter, saving me from having to answer Ava. "Silly little mix-up. For you, I'm happy to do some bumping and rearranging."

"Thanks, Marie." Her voice is sugary sweet again. "I *really* appreciate it. Cute top, by the way."

Marie smiles down at her sleeveless yellow shirt. Ava hands the corrected schedule back to Lois and spins away from the counter.

"What grade?" she asks abruptly, one hand on the door.

"Seventh." I feel my face turn red.

"Me too." After her eyes travel curiously from my face, to my Converse, then back up, she flashes me a quick smile. "See you around."

My chin drops as soon as the door closes behind her. *She's* in seventh grade?

"All set." Momma signs the papers with a flourish and jumps up.

Marie, who reverted back to Ms. Mean Office Lady the second Ava left the room, reviews the forms with a frown. "Ah," she says, pointing to an empty space on the entrance form. "You forgot something."

Momma follows Marie's finger. "Nope. I didn't."

"Father's name and address." Marie looks at Mom suspiciously.

"I'm afraid Ruby's dad moved across the country without leaving a forwarding address, so I don't have that information for you."

Marie blows—and pops—a big green bubble. Then, as though doing us a favor, she collects all the papers in a neat pile, takes them to her desk, and starts tapping her fake fingernails on the keyboard.

A half an hour later, after I've gotten a locker combination, class schedule, campus map, school handbook, ID card, and directions to homeroom, Momma and I finally leave Sweet Citrus Junior High.

My new school. Officially.

"So," Momma says as we walk toward the car. "What'll it be? The beach? Zoo? Movies? Miami? Key West? You name it, we're there."

I can tell she's trying to sound happier than she feels, so I refrain from saying the truth: back to Curly Creek, ASAP. Instead, I settle for what, at the moment, seems to be the next best thing.

"Lemon Grove Mall."

I'm not about to convert to neon, but if I'm really going to be a Sweet Citrus Junior High student, and if Ava is an example of what's to come, a new shirt or two can't hurt.

4. "I've never seen anyone sit so still in one spot for so long before," Momma whispers. "If she weren't surrounded by one-hundred-and-ten-degree air, I'd think she was frozen."

"She's about to move." I hold my breath. "There! Her pencil just tilted to the right."

Momma parts the branches of the indoor tree we're hiding behind and squints for a better look. When Nana Dottie remains motionless, Momma shrugs. "Maybe she fell asleep. Sitting in this heat and listening to the same song for two whole hours is bound to bore anyone enough to nap."

"She hasn't been listening to the same song."

"With the way that piano clatters on, who can tell when one snore-inducing piece ends and the other begins?"

"The more important question," I say, choosing not to point out that some people actually enjoy classical music, "is how are we going to get her attention?"

Momma releases the tree branch and turns to me. "I think you should do it."

"And that makes sense because . . . ?"

"You're her granddaughter."

"You're her daughter—and my *mother*. Isn't it kind of your job to keep me out of harm's way?"

"Sweetie." She puts both hands on my shoulders. "How will I ever be able to keep you out of harm's way if my mother stabs me with her freshly sharpened pencil for interrupting whatever's going on out there?"

I peer through the leaves. "Maybe she's just feeling sad. This could be her way of dealing with everything."

"*Dealing* is devouring a gallon of chocolate chip cookie dough ice cream during an old movie marathon,"

Momma clarifies. "That out there is harnessing negative energy to keep from attacking innocent family members."

I shoot her a look.

"And do you really want to have to borrow paper and a pencil on your first day of school tomorrow?" She wrinkles her nose and shakes her head.

"Fine. But you're not going to be able to hide behind me forever. I'll have to leave for college eventually."

"Road trip!" Momma squeals softly, clapping her hands just loud enough for me to hear.

I can't help smiling as I step out from behind the tree. Nana Dottie doesn't exactly make me feel warm and fuzzy, but I'm not seriously scared of her the way Momma seems to be. And it's not like she's done anything especially scary. She's just kind of quiet, keeps to herself, and does things that Momma and I never do— like sitting in the scorching sun while listening to classical music and working on crossword puzzles.

Still, as I cross the living room and head for the sliding glass door that leads to the patio, I'm a little nervous. What if Nana Dottie really *is* sleeping? Or extremely deep in concentration? Or thinking of Papa Harry? Or anything else that might make her mad at me for interrupting?

Pausing in front of the door, I lift my camera from my chest (where it now sits every day, hanging on a Momma-knitted strap) and sneak a quick shot of Nana Dottie sitting perfectly straight and still.

"Unforgivable."

I've just opened the door and stepped onto the patio, and now I freeze, like the ability to move is immediately snatched from anyone daring enough to venture outside.

"Detestable."

I glance over my shoulder but can't see Momma through the sun's glare on the door and windows. When I turn back, Nana Dottie is staring right at me. Was it the picture? Did she see the camera's flash all the way out here?

"Ten-letter word for 'hateful,' ending in *e*."

Is she asking me or telling me? "Terrible?" I guess.

"Too short." She turns back to the newspaper folded on her lap. "But good try."

I take the sort-of praise as an invitation to move away from the door. After three steps I'm already sweating. How does she do this every day? And why, when there are so many comfortable chairs and sofas inside, in air-conditioning?

"Nana Dottie," I say, knowing I need to focus on the matter at hand, "I don't mean to interrupt, but I had a quick question."

She looks up, her dark eyebrows rising above the top of her sunglasses.

"School starts tomorrow—"

"Your very first day at Sweet Citrus Junior High." As she speaks, the corners of her mouth lift. "It's going to be great. I'm certain of it."

That makes one of us. "Right. I just need a few things, like pencils, paper, maybe some folders . . ."

She rests her pencil on top of the newspaper, pushes her sunglasses on top of her head, and leans forward. "Okay."

"So, I wondered if there was a Walmart nearby? Or some kind of school-supply store?"

"Ruby, you're in Florida now!" she declares, her mouth officially breaking from its straight line into a full smile. "We've got Wal-Mart, Kmart, Target, you name it."

"Great!" I try to sound as excited as she seems to think I should be. "So, if you could just tell us how to get to one of them, Momma and I will be on our way."

Her lips drop. She lowers her sunglasses from the top of her head, sits back in the chair, and takes the pencil and newspaper from her lap. "There's a notepad by the phone in the kitchen. Bring it to me, and I'll write out directions."

I open my mouth to thank her, but then decide against it. She seems upset, but I'm not sure what I said wrong. I turn and head back across the patio. When I reach the sliding door, I pause and watch her reflection in the glass. She's sitting perfectly straight and still again, like I never came outside.

"Nana Dottie?" I turn back to face her. "Would you like to come with us?"

Her lips twitch twice before settling back into a straight line. "I suppose that would be fine."

"Great!" I slide open the door, catch Momma's eye behind the indoor tree leaves, and cock my head to one side. "Maybe we can get ice cream after."

"Ice cream?" Momma mouths, looking worried as she flies out from behind the tree and lands on one of the white leather couches.

"Or a fresh-fruit smoothie." Nana Dottie comes inside and crosses the living room. "Blueberries are antioxidant powerhouses, you know."

As soon as Nana Dottie's back is to us, I steal a quick picture of Momma looking miserable on the couch. She's slumped down so far her head is almost on the seat cushion, and she holds her face in her hands. "Next time, *you* can ask for directions," I whisper once Nana Dottie is out of the room.

"Antioxidant powerhouses?" Momma whines quietly. "Seriously?"

"They can't hurt." I refrain from reminding her that moving here was all her idea. I want to shake her and say that if she never actually talks to Nana Dottie (beyond "Please pass the I Can't Believe It's Not Butter!" at dinner), then we left Curly Creek for nothing.

"Ready?" Nana Dottie stands in the living room doorway, orange purse in one hand, car keys in the other.

"I'll drive," Momma offers as she leaps from the couch.

"School supplies are very important, Francine," Nana Dottie says, lowering her sunglasses over her eyes, "but I'm not about to die for them. That thing you call a car screeches, squeals, and drops what are probably very important mechanical parts every time you pull in and out of the driveway."

Momma looks to me, as though I might be able to defend Nana Dottie's claims as part of the car's charm.

"We'll take the Jag," Nana Dottie says.

I shrug apologetically to Momma and follow Nana Dottie. I haven't been in her car before, but I've seen her drive it in and out of the garage. It's supersleek and shiny, and it looks like it was just driven off the lot . . . so I'm pretty sure it has air-conditioning. And since it's burning up outside and things are sure to get pretty heated inside the car, I'll take all the help I can get.

In the garage, Nana Dottie's big white car sits next to a tiny pineapple-yellow convertible.

"Wow." I open the Jaguar's back door and pause. "What's that?"

"What's what?" Nana Dottie asks.

I point to the convertible.

"Oh." She frowns. "That's Papa Harry's car."

She gets in the Jaguar without another word, so I climb in too and gently close the door. Judging by his car, which is about a third of the size of Nana Dottie's and looks like it only drives at one speed—fast—Papa Harry must've been very fun. Momma's never really talked about him, and whenever I ask any questions, she simply kisses my head, says that sometimes grown-ups do very silly things, and offers to make me a double-decker grilled cheese sandwich.

"I've never been in a convertible before," I say, hoping it's not too late to learn more now. "Do you take it out a lot?"

Nana Dottie removes a lipstick tube from her purse and pouts into the rearview mirror as she applies a fresh shade of pink. "That's Papa Harry's car." She smacks her lips, replaces the tube in her purse, and looks toward the kitchen doorway. "Where's your mother?"

I immediately feel terrible for asking about the convertible and appreciate the change of subject. I open my mouth to say I'm not sure where Momma is—and promptly close it when something starts banging on the other side of the garage door.

"Not very subtle, is she?" Nana Dottie catches my eye in the rearview mirror.

"No." I smile. Momma's many things, but subtle definitely isn't one of them.

Nana Dottie pushes a button above the rearview mirror, and the garage door lifts behind us. Momma stands in the middle of the doorway, her arms filled with cassette tapes, cans of soda, and bags of chips. She steps to the side as Nana Dottie starts the car and backs out of the garage.

Nana Dottie stops next to Momma and rolls down

the front passenger side window. "Francine, really," she says, leaning across the middle console. "You could've waited to clean your car. It isn't going to make any difference."

"I didn't clean." Momma juggles the tapes, cans, and bags until one hand is free to open the door. "I grabbed provisions."

Nana Dottie sits back and brings one palm to her forehead, as though checking for a fever that must be causing her to see what she's seeing. Taking that as her cue to get in, Momma yanks the door open and flops into the passenger seat.

"Leather, huh?" She pats the seat. "Fancy."

"You're letting out the cold air," Nana Dottie says.

Momma closes the door and drops everything in her arms to the floor at her feet. As Momma sits up and buckles her seat belt, Nana Dottie automatically locks all the doors and starts down the driveway.

"So, Ruby," Nana Dottie says brightly, once we're cruising down the palm tree–lined street. "Pencils, paper, and folders?"

"Yes. And maybe an eraser or—"

"What's this?"

I slide forward and peer between the front seats to see what has Momma perplexed.

"What's what?" Nana Dottie's eyes dart from the road to Momma's hand fiddling with the radio.

"Your stereo can hold thirty CDs, but not one tape? Even our car has a tape player."

"New cars don't have tape players, Francine. This car has a CD player, satellite radio, and an iPod adapter. That's enough for most people."

I sit back. In the side view mirror, I can see Momma trying not to pout.

"We'll be gone an hour," Nana Dottie says, her voice gentler. "Surely you can last sixty minutes without that old rock and roll—or carbonated beverages."

Momma's head snaps to the left.

"Have you ever tried cleaning leather?" Nana Dottie continues. "It's not worth the risk. If you become so thirsty it's absolutely unbearable, just tell me and I'll pull off the road."

Momma falls silent, and I stare out the window at the passing palm trees. I'm used to music blaring at top volume, wind whipping my hair around, and yes, the car screeching and squealing while we're driving. Nana Dottie's car is so . . . quiet. The only noise is the air-conditioning whispering through the vents. If I were Nana Dottie and had just lost the most important person in my world, I'd definitely want to surround myself with as much noise as possible.

"Ruby," Nana Dottie says suddenly, as though reading my thoughts and wanting to distract me.

I scoot forward.

"Do you have a computer?"

I glance at Momma, whose face remains blank. "Nope."

Nana Dottie nods and taps her fingers against the steering wheel. "Would you like one?"

Would I like a computer? That goes without saying. The only reason I don't have one is because Momma thinks technology is overrated — and because we could never afford one. I always used one of the two computers at Curly Creek Elementary, or I booked an hour on Curly Creek Library's single laptop when I needed to do research for school or write a paper. But having my own would mean I could e-mail and send Gabby photos whenever I want.

"Absolutely," I say . . .

. . . just as Momma says, "Absolutely not."

"She'll need one for school," Nana Dottie explains. "Kids here have been on the Internet since they were old enough to reach the keyboard."

"And I'm sure the school has many computers for students to use."

"Of course. But Ruby will have homework, and pencils and paper will only get her so far." Nana Dottie shrugs. "It'd be my pleasure to buy it for her."

I wait nervously for Momma's reaction. Going school supply shopping together every year is one of our favorite traditions. I appreciate Nana Dottie's suggestion and certainly wouldn't mind having my very own computer — but not if it upsets Momma and ruins the day.

"Now's not a good time," Momma says.

"Of course it's not," Nana Dottie snaps. "It never is."

As we pull into the Super Walmart parking lot, the quiet hum of the air-conditioning seems to grow louder, and the car seems to get hotter. The air is suddenly so thick, I can't wait for the car to stop. When it does, I throw open the door and hurry into the sweltering, humid haze.

I'm not sure whom to feel worse for. Nana Dottie's obviously very unhappy after losing Papa Harry. Momma tried to do something good by moving to Florida to support Nana Dottie but is now being bossed around like a little kid. And I *am* a kid, and there's nothing I can do to help either of them.

On top of which, I have to deal with my first day at Sweet Citrus Junior High. It's just hours away, and no one seems to realize that a *dozen* new computers won't make it any easier.

5. I've pretended to be sick to get out of school before.

I'm not proud of it, but it's happened on more than one occasion. Like when Mrs. Humboldt, my fifth-grade teacher, announced to the class an upcoming doctor's appointment instead of just surprising us with a substitute, and I came down with a sudden sore throat on the morning of her anticipated absence. Or when Gabby visited her grandparents in Topeka and missed a few days, and I contracted a terrible stomach bug that coincidentally started when she left and ended as soon as she returned. Momma's a smart lady, so I'm pretty sure she knew when I was faking, but she always heated up a can of Campbell's tomato soup and let me stay home anyway. As long as my grades never dropped below a B average, she didn't mind my taking the occasional breather.

Somehow, I don't think she'll let me miss my very first day at Sweet Citrus Junior High . . . but that doesn't keep me from trying.

"Momma, I don't want to alarm you, but I think something's wrong."

"Pacific or Tropical Punch?" She holds up two Capri Sun pouches like she didn't hear me. "What sort of Cooler are you feeling today?"

"That's just it." I slide down in the seat and make my best sick face. My mouth hangs open and my eyelids droop. "I'm not feeling cool. Not at all. I think I have a fever. At least a hundred and eight. Maybe higher."

She lowers the Capri Suns and tilts her head. "A fever several degrees cooler would land you in the hospital. Next time shoot lower." But she leans over the car's middle console and presses her lips to my damp forehead to make sure.

"See?" I say meekly.

"You're warm, but who isn't?" She rummages through the plastic bag in her lap. "You could throw some raw eggs, cheese, and broccoli on the sidewalk and have a quiche in seconds."

"Broccoli?" I shudder.

"Don't worry." She hands me three plastic baggies filled with my favorite cereals: Froot Loops, Golden Grahams, and Lucky Charms. "I had to hide the boxes between towels in the linen closet so your grandmother didn't find them."

"The breakfast of champions!" There's no believing I'm sick now. My smile's too big. "You remembered."

"Of *course* I remembered." Momma scoffs like she's offended I'd think otherwise. "We left Curly Creek, but we did *not* leave our traditions. What kind of mother would I be if I let you loose on your first day without the proper feel-good fuel?"

"Probably the kind who'd try to sneak broccoli into my meals," I say. "What about—"

She reaches into the plastic bag and triumphantly holds up a bottle of chocolate syrup and a canister of Reddi Wip. "Positions, please."

I open the Froot Loops. She holds the syrup over the bag and gives it three good squeezes. When the multicolored cereal is mostly brown, she squirts a dollop of Reddi Wip on top. We repeat the process with the other bags of cereal. Once we're done, I snap the bags shut and squish them with both hands until the cereal crumbles.

"Ready?" Momma clicks the finger holds of a pair of cuticle scissors.

She snips one bottom corner off each bag, and we take turns squeezing the crunchy, chocolaty mush through the holes and into our mouths.

"I almost got low-fat whipped cream," Momma says quietly after several minutes, as if she's confessing that she daydreams of hiding Nana Dottie in the linen closet too.

"We may have to move again," I say, licking my fingers. "The humidity's making you think funny."

"Speaking of funny . . ." Momma swivels in her seat and looks out the window at Sweet Citrus Junior High. It's across the street, and several groups of kids are hanging out on the benches scattered across the lawn, talking and laughing. Four girls on a bench near the street are cracking up, three of them doubled over from something hilarious the fourth said.

"That's not funny," I say. "That's scary."

She turns back to me. I suppress a giggle when I notice her thin chocolate mustache. "What's the worst that can happen?" she asks. "Seriously."

"*Seriously*, I can trip walking up the steps, scrape my hands and knees, bleed all over Ava Grand, stain her designer clothes, get laughed at by the entire school, and spend the whole day crying for Curly Creek in the nurse's office."

Momma frowns, and I think maybe I've got her. Maybe my first-day worst-case scenario is bad enough that she'll let me stay home. At least until we've come up with a solid preventative plan involving tripless shoes, some sort of protective skin covering, or, best of all, a one-way journey back to Kansas.

"That would be bad," she admits. "But I know what could make it better."

"A new-friend machine?" I ask as she unbuckles her seat belt and reaches between the two front seats. "Because unless you have Gabby hidden back there, I'm going to need one of those."

"Close." She hands me the solution to my problems, her smile so wide the chocolate mustache spreads to the bottom of her nose.

"An ABBA lunch box!" I gasp and grab the present. "It's *beautiful*!" And it is. It's ice blue and sparkly, like freshly fallen snow under a late winter sky. Best of all, Agnetha, the band's prettiest member, is pictured on both sides, her arms over her head and a glittery white dress swirling around her.

"Bet no one else will be sitting with their very own Dancing Queen at lunch," Momma says proudly, referring to the group's most popular song — and the one we used to dance to nearly every night in Curly Creek.

"Momma, thank you." I lean over and kiss her cheek. "Really. This is the best first-day present I could've gotten." It might not create friends out of thin air, but it *could* be a great conversation starter that eventually led to friendship. Plus, if I start to feel uncomfortable at any point in the day, I can just look at the pretty pop group and picture Momma singing and dancing to her old album at home. That always makes me feel better.

"What about you?" I look up suddenly. She still has a chocolate mustache, but I don't feel like laughing now.

"What about me?"

"I'll be gone all day. Will you be okay? Alone in that big house . . . with Nana Dottie?"

"Oh, sure!" She waves one hand, like I'm silly to be concerned. "We're going to write tiny letters in tiny boxes in the blazing-hot sun, pretend to listen to boring music as we nap with our eyes open, and if we're really lucky, race each other to see who can name all of the world's vegetables in order of most nutritious to least. It'll be a *hoot*."

I pause. "My money's on Nana Dottie to win that race."

"Mine too." She pats my knee. "I'll be fine. Thank you. Now what do you say? Are you ready to show these sun-heads what the Midwest's made of?"

I'm still not sure, but I don't really have a choice. The groups of kids are slowly standing and heading for the front door. I'm already the new girl; I don't want to be late too.

"I can do it," I say when she starts to open her door. "Go alone, I mean."

She sits back. For just a second, her blue eyes are confused—almost sad. "But I always walk you in on the first day."

"I know." I search my brain for an explanation. I loved having Momma walk me in to school in Kansas, where everyone else's parents did the same thing. But I can already guess that being escorted by Momma into Sweet Citrus Junior High is a surefire way to get noticed—and not in a good way. "It's just—"

"You know what? Never mind. I get it." She reaches over and grabs me in a tight hug. "Have a wonderful day. Be yourself. And remember, Coconut Grove isn't any different from Curly Creek. You're one of a kind — the *best* kind — wherever you are."

For some reason this makes me feel like crying, so I hug her back, then gently pull away. I give myself a quick once-over, even though there's nothing much I can do about my appearance at this point, and take a deep breath. I open the door just as the first bell rings.

"Gotta go!" I hoist my backpack onto my shoulders, hug my ABBA lunch box to my chest, and hip-check the door closed. "Have fun, but save some for me!"

I round the back of the car and wait for a break in traffic before running across the street. I wave to Momma as soon as I reach the lawn. She blows me a kiss and starts the car, which slowly grumbles to life. As she pulls away from the curb, the muffler burps, leaving behind a thick black cloud.

"Excuse you," a voice says from behind me.

My shoulders slump. Really? This is *really* how my

day's going to start? With bodily function jokes I haven't heard since the third grade?

"It's an old car," I say reluctantly, turning around. "My momma . . ."

I stop. Ava Grand stands before me. She's smiling, but the expression is more "Poor new girl doesn't stand a chance" than "Welcome to Sweet Citrus." This greeting is enough to send me sprinting in the opposite direction, but I'm too distracted by Ava's outfit to move. She's wearing a long white sundress, silver sandals, and a sparkly silver scarf looped loosely around her neck. Her accessories include silver hoop earrings and at least a dozen silver bangle bracelets lining her left arm. As she switches her silver leather tote bag from one shoulder to the other, her long hair sways behind her back, and the bracelets jingle like some sort of magical musical instrument.

Ava Grand is a modern-day Dancing Queen.

"I'm sorry," she says.

"Oh." I smile. She was kidding. Maybe that's just how kids break the ice here. "That's okay. It *is* a noisy car. Nana Dottie says she can hear us coming ten minutes before she sees us."

Ava's sky-blue eyes flick quickly to the right, where three girls stand in a straight line, as if waiting for their cue. They're all wearing sundresses and metallic sandals, and they're using grown-up purses instead of backpacks to carry their books.

None of the papers Marie the mean office lady gave us mentioned a dress code. I wish they had, because right now I feel pretty silly in my new denim shorts, yellow T-shirt, and old red Converse. I also wish my ears were pierced, since my only accessory is a thin green belt Momma knitted last night.

"I meant . . . *sorry*?" Ava cups one hand against her ear. "I didn't quite catch that. Did you just say *Momma*?"

"And *Nana Dottie*?" one of the backup dancers adds.

Ava's smile grows as she starts walking toward the school steps, her friends in tow.

"By the way," she calls over her shoulder, "love your shirt!"

I look down. Momma and I spent hours trying

to find the perfect top to wear with my new shorts. I wanted something fun but not crazy. Different but not strange. We finally decided on this one — a yellow T-shirt with SOUTH BEACH printed in gold block letters around a glowing orange sun — after dismissing countless others. We were sure it did everything I wanted my new first-day shirt to do.

Apparently, we were wrong.

I follow the crowd down the walkway leading to Sweet Citrus Junior High. I know I should probably look around and take mental notes on what everyone else is wearing so I don't make the same mistake twice. But I can't. My eyes stay locked on my red Converse the whole way. I love these sneakers. They're worn. They're comfortable. They make me think of Gabby, who has an identical pair. And if I can just concentrate hard enough, maybe they'll take me home the way Dorothy's ruby slippers did for her.

"Well, hello to you, too, Kansas!"

At least I think that's what Mr. Fox says. It's hard to hear him — or anything else — over the shrill, frantic beeping overhead.

"What?" I shout and cover my ears at the same time.

He's standing inside the building, a few feet from the entrance. He motions for me to back up, which makes me realize I've stopped walking. I was so focused on my sneakers I didn't notice the ground beneath them change as they left the walkway, climbed steps, and stopped. I look up now and see I'm standing in one of the big gray boxes that fit the front doors like puzzle pieces.

I stumble backward and the beeping stops.

"New girl knows how to make an entrance." Mr. Fox chuckles as he weaves through the surrounding students. "Nice haircut, Batman. Sweet kicks, Sprout."

I frown. Mr. Fox exchanges high and low fives with several kids as he moves toward the metal detectors. He seems to like the kids and they seem to like him . . . so why is he trying to embarrass *me*?

"What do you say we try that again?"

Mr. Fox looks at me. So do about a hundred of my new classmates. I'd really like to continue backing up, all the way down the front lawn, across the street, and right into the ocean, but doing so would require pushing through the crowd behind me. Which means I can go in only one direction.

Forward.

The metal detector screams before I can pass all the way through. I jump back. Behind me, in front of me, pushing up beside me, kids laugh and cheer. They seem to be eager for a show rather than eager to mortify me specifically, but I'm still tempted to curl up in my lunch box until dinner.

My lunch box. My beautiful ABBA lunch box. It's made of metal.

I look at Mr. Fox. He's smiling. He's already figured out what's setting off the detector and is waiting for me to make the connection. I reluctantly relax my arms and am only vaguely aware of people pushing against me as they try to get a glimpse of what dangerous item is about to be confiscated by security.

The beeping only lasts a second before Mr. Fox holds my Dancing Queen in his hands.

"Will I get it back?" I ask as soon as I pass through the metal detector. "*Please*, can I get it back? My momma just gave it to me this morning and—"

"Is that . . . ?

"It couldn't be."

"I haven't seen one of those since preschool."

The heat in my cheeks travels up my forehead and down my neck. It's a good thing I won't be wearing this shirt again, since it'll probably be permanently sweat-stained after today. I turn slowly and am not even a little surprised to see Ava Grand and her backup dancers standing in front of the crowd. Now that I've made it through, the laughter and cheering fades. Everyone hears what Ava says next.

"It *is*." She puts one hand to her chest, like Momma's gift is a fluffy, adorable kitten. "It's a lunch box. Just like the ones we used when we were little kids." She steps away from her friends and puts one hand on my shoulder. "Are you all that far behind? In—where is it again? Mars? Venus?"

"Kansas," I say quietly, looking down at my Converse.

I'm afraid she'll make me say it louder, but the bell rings again before she can.

"Show's over, munchkins!" Mr. Fox declares. "Let's move it."

I don't look up as the crowd migrates down the hall. The lobby grows quiet, and even though I know I'm officially late, I don't move. I'm still staring at my sneakers when my beautiful ABBA lunch box appears inches from my face.

"Enjoy your first day," Mr. Fox says.

6. "So Andy dares Brian, and Brian dares Clint, and Clint dares Justin, and around and around it goes until Andy tells Brian that if he's that scared of getting caught, he should probably sit with the girls at recess, which of *course* makes Brian more determined than ever, so he finally does it . . . and you'll never guess what happens next."

"He gets caught?" I smile at the excitement in Gabby's voice.

"Not just caught—busted. Like, empty-the-trash-cans-and-clean-the-blackboards-every-day-for-a-week busted. Mrs. Hamilton came in while he was turning her desk upside down, and he was so scared he lost his grip, dropped the desk, and broke her favorite red pen that was in the top drawer."

"Wow. He really earned that punishment."

"Definitely." Gabby giggles, then groans. "I *so* wish you could've been there to see it! That was the only first first-day prank you've missed in—"

"Forever. I know. I wish I could've been there too."

"Anyway, enough about me. Tell me about *you*. I want to know everything. What's your school like? How are your teachers? Are the kids nice? What are they into? Do you like any of them half as much as you like me?"

"Not even close," I say truthfully.

Picking up on my tone the way only a best friend can, Gabby pauses. "What about everything else? Was it bad?"

"Not bad." I lower the back of the lounge chair until I'm lying completely flat. "Awful. Terrible. Miserable. Easily the worst day of my life."

"Oh, Ruby. I'm so sorry. But it'll get better, right? I

mean, every first day in a new place is rough. Not that I know from personal experience, but remember when Parker Jameson moved here from Oklahoma? He cried on his first day. Seriously bawled like a baby in front of the whole class."

"We were in first grade. Parker Jameson was six. If I were six and cried today, I don't think I'd beat myself up over it."

"*Did* you cry today?"

"No, thankfully. But I did dress like a tourist, get lost on the way to six of my seven classes, circle the cafeteria for forty-three minutes without sitting down, trip on the school steps, and nearly get run over by a two-person bicycle while crossing the street to Momma's car. Oh, and that's another thing—kids don't call their mommas 'momma' here."

"What do they call them?"

"Mary. Betty. Granter of My Every Wish and Command."

"Not so catchy."

"No." Too drained to lift my head, I reach down and feel around the tile for my Yoo-hoo. "Anyway, it stunk.

But it's over. And the good news is that tomorrow can't be worse."

"Hang on," Gabby says, and then talks quietly with someone in the background. She comes back several seconds later. "Ruby, I'm so, so sorry, but—"

"You have to go." I checked the kitchen clock when I took the cordless phone outside. I knew we wouldn't have much time, but some was better than none. "Heading down for some Cannonball Creek?"

"It's going to be crazy. Tracy's dad made a special inner tube with an extra-wide hole out of tarps and balloons, so we're going to use it as a target and have a contest to see who can score the most bull's-eyes in five minutes, and whoever wins gets . . ."

I'm gulping Yoo-hoo so fast the bottle's empty in seconds. "Gets what?" I ask, wiping my mouth with the back of my hand.

"I'm doing it again. You had an awful, terrible, miserable day, and I keep rattling on about these ridiculous things."

"They're not ridiculous. They're traditions."

"Same thing when your best friend's unhappy a million miles away."

I smile. As bad as today was, as bad as tomorrow and the next day might be, I still have Gabby. Even if she is a million miles away.

"I really have to go," she says, "but I love you and miss you and wish you were here. So much."

"Me too. Tell everyone I said hi. Talk tomorrow."

I hang up and rest the phone on my stomach. It's almost six o'clock, and it's still as hot as it was when the sun was directly overhead. I was too tired to shower when I got home a few hours ago, so I thought I'd just jump in the pool to cool off . . . but I didn't have the energy for that either. I'm not sure *what* I have energy for, besides lying here and imagining what everyone's doing back home.

"Aloha!"

Momma, however, has other ideas.

"Where'd you get the guitar?" I ask.

"This isn't a guitar!" She strums the strings like she's Steven Tyler, her favorite rock star. "It's a ukulele."

I sit up on my elbows. "A you-ka—"

"Lay-lee." She finishes with two strums.

"Momma," I say, choosing my words carefully, "did you know Florida is home to the biggest box of Cracker Jack? Is that the real reason we moved here?"

She stops strumming and perches on the edge of my lounge chair. "Florida's home to the biggest box of Cracker Jack? Did you learn that in school today? How big is this box? Do you have a map?"

I raise my eyebrows at the hula skirt, purple lei, and plastic coconut bra she's wearing over her bathing suit. "Your outfit looks like it's made out of Cracker Jack prizes. You look like one of those hula girls people stick on their dashboards."

"Thanks, sweetie!" She kisses my head and jumps up. "I didn't think I'd make it to Honolulu and back before you got out of school, so I went to this magical Floridian land called Party Palace."

"Where grass skirts grow on trees?"

"Isn't it great?" She twirls and the green strands float around her waist. "And don't worry—I got you one too!"

I laugh as she pulls another skirt, a pink lei, and a

plastic coconut bra from a big shopping bag. "Thanks, Momma . . . but what exactly am I supposed to do with this tropical ensemble?"

She holds out one hand to pull me up. "It's six o'clock on your first day of school."

I lift my hair out from under the lei after she's placed it around my neck. "And?"

"And what do we always do at six o'clock on your first day of school?"

I was almost beginning to feel better, but remembering what we're missing makes the pain come rushing back. "We go cannonballing in Curly Creek with Gabby, Mrs. Kibben, and all our friends."

"Right." She wraps the skirt around my waist. "Now, unlike the breakfast of champions, that tradition's tough to duplicate here since we don't have a creek —"

"Or friends."

"So *instead*, I thought we'd start a new one." She ties the plastic coconut bra over my T-shirt and turns me around. "Aloha!"

My chin drops. I must've still been staring at my

Converse when I came outside, because that's the only way I could've missed the "First Annual Coconut Grove Luau and Sand Castle Carving Contest" set up on the other side of the pool. Nana Dottie's patio set has been replaced by a tiki hut surrounded by white sand. Orange lanterns are strung between tiki torches and inflatable palm trees. Striped beach chairs sit beneath a pink beach umbrella, and a small, short table between them holds two topless pineapples with curly straws. A banner bearing the party's official name is taped on the fence behind the hut above a poster of the sun setting over turquoise water.

"Party Palace sells sand?" I'm so surprised, it's the first thing I think to say.

"No, unfortunately. It took two plastic buckets and eighteen trips to carry that much from the beach to the car."

She dashes around the pool, her grass skirt flying behind her. As she puts on hula music and lights torches, I take it all in. I think about how hard she must've worked to pull off this new tradition. I think about everything that happened at school and how none of it seems completely catastrophic right now, in this moment, at the First Annual Coconut Grove Luau and Sand Castle Carving Contest.

After all, Ava Grand might have fancy clothes, pierced ears, and three best friends . . . but she doesn't have Momma.

"Where are you going?" she calls after me as I start jogging toward the back door.

I glance over my shoulder to see her carrying a big plastic bin, which, I assume, holds the wet sand that will soon become a castle. "I'll be right back. Just want to get my camera!"

I slow from a jog to a walk once I'm inside the house. It's totally silent; I can't even hear the hula music playing outside. I haven't seen Nana Dottie since I got home from school, when she invited me to talk about my day over a platter of skinny crackers and something beige and mushy she called hummus and I politely declined. She might be working on her crosswords now. Or napping. I don't want to disturb her by clopping like a horse across the marble floor.

I make it to my room as quickly and quietly as I can, grab my camera from the bed, and hurry back to the living room. Through the tall windows I see Momma dancing in the sand as she straightens the inflatable palm trees. I'm about to slide open the door when the silence breaks inside the house.

I hold my breath and wait. Maybe it was me. Maybe I was too busy watching Momma I didn't realize my camera knocked against the glass door or my sneakers squeaked on the floor.

But there it is again. It's some kind of rattling, like dice rolling across the table during Yahtzee. And it sounds like it's coming from the kitchen.

Did Momma invite Nana Dottie to the luau? If so, did Nana Dottie decline the invitation, just like I declined hers earlier? Deciding it's worth making sure, since I don't want to hurt Nana Dottie's feelings, I tiptoe across the room.

"Fifty-eight."

I freeze in the hallway. That definitely didn't sound like my grandma.

"Which brings you up to two hundred and eleven. Nicely done."

My eyes widen. Unless Nana Dottie caught a bad cold that deepened her voice several octaves over the past two hours, that's *not* my grandma.

It's a man.

The rattling starts again, and I tiptoe to the kitchen doorway. Nana Dottie's back is to me. She's sitting at the kitchen table, across from a younger man with a dark tan and black hair. She shakes a red felt pouch, reaches in with one hand, pulls something out, and places the pouch on the table next to a square board.

They're playing a game, but it's not noisy enough to be Yahtzee. I step into the room and lean forward to try to read the box on the floor.

"Well, aloha," the man says.

I grab the kitchen counter to keep from falling over. Clearly, this greeting's meant for me. "Hi."

Nana Dottie swivels in her chair. Her eyes travel up slowly from my Converse to my chest. "Ruby? What on earth are you wearing? Are those . . . coconuts?"

I'm fully clothed underneath my hula-girl outfit, but I suddenly feel naked. "Momma's throwing a luau in honor of my first day at Sweet Citrus Junior High."

"A luau?" Nana Dottie's face twists. "Where does she think she is? And what kind of way is that to spend your first school night? Surely you have homework."

"I don't, actually." It's true. I always had at least a reading assignment after the first day of school at Curly Creek, but Sweet Citrus teachers apparently like to give their students a few days to warm up to the idea of homework. "Would you like to join us? I'm sure there's enough sand for everyone."

"*Sand?*" Nana Dottie half stands from her chair and tilts toward the window facing the backyard.

"I'm Oscar," the man says with a wave. "Nice camera."

"Oh." I'd forgotten I was holding it. "Thanks."

The doorbell rings. Nana Dottie's so distracted by the scene outside, I don't think she hears it. "Do you want me to—"

"Got it!" Momma shouts, coming into the house.

I smile as the back door slams shut and her bare feet slap against the living room floor. Unlike me, she doesn't care who hears her.

"Whew! That was a challenge, let me tell you." Momma's voice grows louder as she nears the kitchen. "Would you believe they'd never heard of Hawaiian pizza? I had to tell them exactly how to make it, with—"

She stops in the doorway.

"Good grief, Francine." Nana Dottie shakes her head as she gives Momma the same once-over she gave me. "It's the first day of school, not Halloween. What kind of example are you setting for your daughter?"

My eyes shift to Momma. She doesn't embarrass easily, but her face is cherry red as she stares at the top of the pizza box. I frantically try to think of something to say, something that will make both Momma and Nana Dottie feel better. But my brain must still be recharging from the day, because it draws a blank.

"Ham."

Momma looks up. I look at Oscar.

"And pineapple—in rings, not cubes." He shrugs.

"Everyone who's anyone knows that's how you make a Hawaiian pizza."

He smiles at Momma, which makes me smile. Nana Dottie's still shaking her head and now she closes her eyes, like she can't believe Oscar would stoop so low.

"Right," Momma says. The corners of her mouth lift only slightly before dropping again. "Ruby? Shall we?"

"It was nice to meet you," I say before hurrying after Momma. When I'm halfway down the hall, I spin around and dash back to the kitchen. I take two quick pictures before Nana Dottie and Oscar even know I'm there, and then spin around again.

When I reach the patio, Momma's in the tiki hut, cutting the Hawaiian pizza like it's made of wood and not dough.

"Oscar seems nice, doesn't he?" I hold the pizza box in place as she saws. "And I think he thinks you're pretty. Did you see the way he smiled at you, like—"

"Like my outfit's made of Cracker Jack prizes? Or like I fell off a dusty dashboard?"

I frown. She sounds annoyed—almost mad. "Momma,

I promise I wasn't making fun before. I think this—all of it—is amazing. It was so nice of you to go to so much trouble, and I really appreciate it."

Momma puts down the knife. She takes a deep breath and offers a small smile. "I know you do. Making you happy is my greatest joy, and I didn't mean to snap. It's just . . . your grandmother knows how to push buttons I never knew I had."

I look around. The sun is setting, and the paper lanterns glow softly in the darkening light. The inflatable palm trees sway in the warm breeze. The hula music still plays. The sand cubes sit in front of the beach chairs, awaiting artful transformation.

We had a minor setback . . . but the party must go on.

"I'm hot," I announce suddenly.

"You are?" Momma's eyebrows furrow in concern. "Do you want to cool off in the air-conditioning? Or take a cold shower?"

"That's okay. I'll be fine in a few seconds." I kick off my Converse and take off my socks, but leave on everything else. "We both will."

She looks at me. I look at the pool.

"Ruby Lee," Momma says, and I can hear the smile in her voice. "You are your mother's daughter."

"Thank goodness for that."

And then we cannonball into the pool, grass skirts, coconut bras, and all.

7. Now that I know how to get to homeroom,
I take my time getting there the next day.
I sit on a bench until the last group of
students reaches the metal detectors. Once they start
passing through, I dash across the lawn and sprint up
the steps.

"Morning, Mr. Fox." I stop outside the door and try
to catch my breath.

"Good morning, Miss Dorothy! I see we survived
the first day."

"Barely." I slide my backpack in front of me. I

remove my lunch box and camera, which I now carry with me everywhere, and reach them through the doorway. The metal detector beeps four times before Mr. Fox pulls them out of range. I reach my hands back through.

"If you're wearing invisible metal rings, the machine's not picking them up." Mr. Fox eyes my wiggling fingers.

"Would you mind if we try that again?" I ask.

He looks down at the lunch box and camera, and then at me. "What's wrong with the way we just did it?"

"It was too slow."

"If you're worried about being late, trying again won't help." He starts to open the lunch box — apparently to make sure I'm not using it to conceal other, more dangerous weapons. "You might want to ask your mom to bring you a few minutes earlier tomorrow."

I lower my hands to my sides. "Mr. Fox, have you ever been the new kid?"

He raises his eyes and lifts his chin, like he's trying to recall that far back.

"It's hard," I say, since I don't know how far back he's going or how long it'll take, and I do have to get to homeroom. "But I think the key is to blend in as soon as possible."

"And I don't suppose the metal detectors are helping that cause."

"No, sir. It's hard to go unnoticed when your lunch makes you look like a criminal every day. The faster I get my stuff through the doors, the fewer times the detectors will beep, and the less attention I'll get."

"Miss Dorothy, I'm happy to help . . . but why don't you bring your lunch in a paper sack? Or buy it here, the way most kids do?"

He moves his hands as he talks. The motion makes the Dancing Queen sparkle—and me smile.

"Because, Mr. Fox . . . I guess I'm just not like most kids."

This seems to please him. He winks at me, then thrusts the lunch box and camera through the door like they're on fire and I have an extinguisher. The metal detector beeps three times. I shove them back, and he grabs them. The metal detector beeps twice. We try it two more times. On the fourth try, the metal detector manages a half beep you wouldn't hear in a crowd of kids unless you were really listening for it.

"Perfect." I grin. "Thank you."

I check the sunburst clock hanging on the wall next to the doors as I hurry into the building. I still have two minutes before the last bell, so I swing by the girls' restroom just off the lobby. I noticed it yesterday and figured it might be quieter than the main one, which coincidentally separates my locker from Ava Grand's and seems to serve as her personal lounge.

I'm right—it's empty. It's a small room without stalls, so I lock the door before resting my backpack on the floor and facing the mirror.

"Today will be better," I quietly tell my reflection, which doesn't look convinced. "It *has* to be better."

One of Momma's favorite mottos is "Kill them with kindness." Which means if someone's giving you trouble, your best retaliation is to be as sweet as sugar until that someone stops. Momma had muttered this phrase during our drive to school this morning when a red sports car cut her off while getting on the highway and made her drop her iced coffee. The driver zoomed away without looking back, but Momma waved and called "Have a great morning!" through her open window anyway.

And I've decided that's the perfect way to get through today. No matter what Ava Grand says or does to embarrass me, I'll thank her and give her a compliment. Guessing that might be challenging in the heat of the moment, I already started a list on the palm of my hand. So far it includes her pretty hair, nice dress, and commanding presence. (I almost wrote "demanding presence" first, since that seemed more accurate, but then thought that might not go over as well.)

I turn from side to side in front of the mirror. It took twenty minutes to get ready this morning—twice as long as usual—and I'm still not sure I did it right. I passed on the only dress I own, a short denim jumper covered in purple butterflies, because it makes me look younger, not older like Ava's and her friends' dresses do for them. My other new clothes included a pair of white jeans and four shirts like the South Beach one but featuring different towns like Miami, Coral Gables, and Key West.

The shirts were out, but I thought the jeans could work; I didn't see one girl in jeans yesterday, but most of the boys wore them, so at least they were acceptable. After careful consideration, I paired an old, but still bright red, tank top with the jeans.

There wasn't anything I could do about my ears between yesterday and today, so I left my hair down to make it harder to see that they aren't pierced. And neither Momma nor I own makeup, but I do have an old lip balm that smells and tastes like cookie dough, which I put on.

Now there's just one thing missing.

I double-check the door to make sure it's locked, then take my old plastic Walkman from my backpack. Satisfied no one will barge in on me, I put on the headphones, crank the volume . . . and press play.

"Dancing Queen" explodes in my head. I wiggle, spin, and sway to the music with my eyes closed. I feel a little silly at first but do my best to pretend I'm in our living room in Curly Creek instead of in a bathroom at Sweet Citrus Junior High. I relax a little more with every note, and by the time the song ends, I feel strong, confident, and like I can handle anything that happens today.

The last morning bell rings just as the final note fades. I grab my backpack, unlock and throw open the door, and sprint to homeroom.

I feel twenty pairs of eyes on me as I enter the room and walk to my desk. I tell myself to meet at least one or two of them and smile, but I don't. I can't. My Converse have once again become the center of the earth, pulling my eyes down with some sort of gravitational force. I don't look up until I sit down and my feet disappear.

"Nice headband, Venus," a voice says from behind me.

My breath catches as I realize I'm still wearing my Walkman. I was so startled by the bell that I forgot to take it off before running out of the bathroom. Now everyone can see that I still listen to cassette tapes, which I know must be ancient because Momma and I always buy them used at Mr. Lou's Junk 'n' Treasures.

"Mars."

I yank off the headphones, open my backpack, and swap the Walkman for a notebook.

"Jupiter?"

I'm about to continue a note to Gabby but stop at the third planet. I'm pretty sure my face is the same color as my shirt as I look over my shoulder. Ava Grand's smile is small and thin. It's the kind that holds back laughter.

"Kansas," I say, wincing when my voice cracks on the second syllable.

Her lips part, and a giggle escapes. She turns toward her friends, whose desks surround hers, and shakes her head like she can't believe what she just heard and wants to make sure they heard it too.

The final bell rings and I turn back. Mr. Soto, our homeroom teacher, leads us through the Pledge of Allegiance and takes attendance. Ten minutes pass rather uneventfully, and I'm about to tell Gabby as much in my letter to her when the classroom door flies open.

My pencil stops. The room falls silent. Twenty-two pairs of eyes—mine and Mr. Soto's included—lock onto the woman floating before us. She's tall and thin, with shiny black hair that hangs straight to the middle of her back and thick, square-cut bangs. Her eyes are shielded by round ivory sunglasses. She wears a sleeveless peach shirt and a matching skirt made of a light, shimmery material that falls to her ankles and swooshes around her legs as she glides to the front of the room.

We're too awed to move.

She glides by Mr. Soto's desk. A short man in a white suit and peach bow tie dashes into the room next; his white dress shoes squeak on the linoleum as he skids to a stop next to her. The man's presence unfreezes Mr. Soto, who seems to suddenly remember why the pair's here and returns his attention to his attendance book.

The short man pulls a white rectangular device from the inside pocket of his sports coat. He sticks another device on top of the first and presses a button.

I jump as the room fills with music. It's unlike any I've ever heard, with a loud, fast beat and a choppy melody. Someone sings, but the voice is so screechy and distorted, I can't make out actual words. The sound pierces my ears—and not in a good way—so I'm surprised when everyone else seems to enjoy it. A quick scan of the room shows my classmates bobbing their heads and tapping their feet.

When it ends, the silence that follows is louder than the music that just played. The woman takes a deep breath, holds it, and exhales dramatically. She twirls around and glides back across the room. I think she just might float through the closed door like a ghost, but then she pauses two inches in front of it.

"Citrus Star," she says without looking at us. "Countdown to celebrity: twenty-eight days."

The short man reaches around her and pushes open the door. "Details to follow via e-mail," he says.

The room explodes as soon as the door closes behind them. Desks push together. Small groups form. Excited discussion ensues. I have no idea what's going on and am just starting to panic when Mr. Soto raps a ruler on his desk.

"You heard Miss Anita," he shouts over the buzz. "You have four weeks until you share your talents with the entire school. I don't need to tell you what a significant opportunity this is, so prepare wisely."

"Excuse me," I say to the boy at the desk next to mine as the bell rings. Everyone else has already bolted for the door, excited to continue their discussions outside the classroom. I'd like to bolt too—preferably back to my personal restroom—but I can't risk not knowing what's obviously very important information. The last thing I need is to be out of the loop even more than I already am. "What just happened? What's Citrus Star?"

He sighs. "Citrus Star is an annual embarrassing display of ego that many of our classmates prepare for all summer. It's the school's version of *American Idol*, *America's Got Talent*, and a variety of other ridiculous time-wasters."

American Idol? *America's Got Talent*? What's he talking about?

"It's a glorified talent show," he explains.

"Oh!" I'm so relieved I smile. We had talent shows in Curly Creek too. I couldn't sing or dance worth a lick so never got onstage myself, but I always enjoyed attending.

"Participation's mandatory."

My smile drops. "Oh."

"Exactly." He shoves the book he'd been reading into his backpack and stands up. "You're new, right?"

I hesitate, then nod. "My name's Ruby. I just moved here from Kansas."

"Kansas," he repeats thoughtfully. "Amelia Earhart. Charlie Parker. Vivian Vance."

I wait for Dorothy Gale to follow in this list of famous Kansans, but he stops there. "You know Vivian Vance?" I ask. *I* know Vivian Vance because she played the funny neighbor in *I Love Lucy*, a really old TV show Momma watches on video. But I didn't think anyone else my age from anywhere outside the Kansas border did.

"Nice state," he says instead of answering my question. "Talented people."

"Thanks," I say, even though I'm definitely not one of them.

He starts walking, so I quickly get my stuff together. I don't remember him being in my first-period class yesterday, but maybe his is near mine. Maybe we can walk to the locker hallway together. Maybe he can answer some of my other questions, like why all the girls at Sweet Citrus Junior High look like they should be in high school, or why Ava seems to hate me without even knowing me, or where else you can spend lunch besides the cliquey cafeteria.

"So do you know what you're going to do?" I ask as I zip up my backpack. "Sing? Dance? Juggle?"

I look up when he doesn't answer.

The room's empty. He's gone, and I'm alone. Again.

8. "Sweetie, would you please hand me another skein of green?"

"Momma, the basket of yarn is by your feet. I'm on the other side of the room."

"I have a really good rhythm going. I don't want to mess it up."

I turn around. She's sprawled out on the white leather couch. A half-finished blanket's on her lap—and so are her knitting needles. "I can see why."

She shoots up and leans forward, happy to have my attention. "Want to go swimming? Or watch a movie?

Or go swimming and watch a movie? Not at the same time, but one after the other?"

"Absolutely. Right after I figure this out."

She groans as I turn back to the laptop. "But you've been doing that for an *hour*. At this rate you may not be ready till tomorrow, and I'm very busy tomorrow."

"Busy?" I turn around again. As far as I knew, the busiest day Momma's had since our arrival was when she planned the luau. "Doing what?"

"Yes. Doing what?"

I look up. Nana Dottie stands in the living room doorway, arms crossed over her chest. "Hi, Nana Dottie," I say, since Momma's already trying to disappear into the couch.

"Hello, Ruby." She leaves the doorway, walks around the couch, and perches on the piano bench. "How was school today?"

"Fine. You'll be happy to know that three of my teachers assigned homework, which I've already finished."

"You're right. That does make me happy." She smiles

and looks like she wants to say something else, but she's not sure what. "Good girl."

I don't know if she's praising me because I already finished my assignments, because I paid enough attention to know that it would make her happy, or because the combination actually *does* make her happy. I don't wonder for long, though, since the feeling doesn't seem to last.

"What are you doing tomorrow?" Nana Dottie asks Momma. Her smile is gone.

"Stuff," Momma says, picking at imaginary pulls in the blanket on her lap.

"What kind of stuff?"

"*Stuff*, stuff. My stuff. Personal stuff."

I frown. Momma sounds like me when I'm cranky and don't feel like doing something she's asked me to do.

"It's a simple question, Francine. I'm just making conversation."

"Sure you are."

Momma mumbles this last part, and I hope Nana Dottie doesn't hear it. I sneak a peek at the piano bench to check, and see her lips purse and eyes narrow.

"Excuse me for being concerned. But you've been here three weeks, and I haven't seen you do much more than swim, shop, and play. This is your life now, Francine. Not a vacation."

"I know that," Momma snaps. "We're settling. Adjusting. I'm not going to abandon Ruby before she's completely comfortable."

"Since when is getting a job abandonment?" Nana Dottie asks. "Ruby's in school for seven hours a day. What can you do for her then?"

"Make sure nothing keeps me from being in front of that school ten minutes before the last bell rings so that she doesn't have to wait. Plan fun, relaxing evenings to help her unwind."

"She's not a music box. She's a young adult—a sharp, capable one at that. And she can take the bus home. Or I can pick her up. I'd be happy to pick her up."

Despite our careful SPF 50 application, Momma's face looks like it's been baking in the sun all day.

"I'm fine either way," I say quickly. "I love that you pick me up, Momma, but I'd also be perfectly willing to take the bus or ride with Nana Dottie, if that's easier."

"It's not," Momma says.

There's a long, awkward silence. I'm tempted to break it but don't want Momma to think I'm taking Nana Dottie's side by moving the moment along. Momma seems pretty irritated right now, and it's obvious she wants Nana Dottie to know it.

"Caroline, the wonderful receptionist at my club, is having a baby," Nana Dottie finally says.

I raise my eyebrows. This is an unexpected—but appreciated—change of topic.

"Isn't that nice." The politeness in Momma's voice is strained.

"Is she having a boy or a girl?" I ask, wanting them both to know that ignoring the awkwardness is A-OK with me.

Nana Dottie gives me a small smile. "She doesn't know yet. She wants to be surprised."

"That's a pretty risky surprise," I say. "How will she

decorate the nursery? Or know what clothes to buy? She doesn't want her little boy to be dressed in pink or her little girl to be dressed in blue, does she? I guess there's always yellow. And light green would probably work. Still, I think I'd want to know. You wanted to know too, didn't you, Momma? You knew I was a girl before you had me?"

"Yes, Ruby," Momma says, her voice warmer. "I knew."

"I knew too," Nana Dottie adds. "I went on a shopping spree for pink Onesies, dresses, bibs, and shoes as soon as your mother told me. I sent boxes and boxes of beautiful little-girl clothes before you were born. And every year, right before your birthday, I sent more."

"Really? Thanks, Nana." I smile. "That was so nice of you."

Nana Dottie's hot-pink lips immediately set in a straight line, and though I didn't mean to upset her, I can guess why I did.

She assumed I knew about the boxes when, really,

this is the first I've heard of them. I always got a present from Nana Dottie every birthday and Christmas, but it was usually a single sweater or pair of pajamas—never an entire box of clothes. Momma clearly had kept this from me. Why she did, I don't have a clue.

"Anyway," Nana Dottie says, "Caroline will be on maternity leave beginning next week. She'll be out seven months, perhaps longer."

"Good for her," Momma says. "All mothers-to-be should have that option. Pregnancy can be brutal. No offense, Rubes."

"None taken. Besides, I'm sure I've more than made up for it by now."

"And then some." Momma winks.

I relax. This is good. We hit a small rough patch, but that's to be expected. Like Momma said—we're settling. Adjusting. Nana Dottie's doing the same thing. The situation's new for all of us, and it'll take some time before we're completely at ease with one another. As long as we talk, as long as we *try*, then we're on the right track.

"How are you on the phone?"

My head snaps toward Nana Dottie, who's looking at Momma.

"I mean, with people other than your mother," she continues. "I know those skills could use improvement."

Momma's cheeks glow pink, then red, then purple. "What do you mean?"

"You had a job in Curly Creek, did you not? At that—what was it? Spa? Salon?"

"Nail boutique." Momma speaks, but somehow, her lips don't move.

"She was great on the phone there," I offer, since Momma looks like a volcano on the brink of eruption. "I stopped by after school a lot, and she was always friendly, courteous, and professional. And she's one of the best multitaskers I've ever seen. She could juggle a phone, date book, and nail file all at the same time."

I'm smiling because I really am that proud of Momma and think Nana Dottie will be too . . . but then she frowns. And I wonder what I said wrong.

"You stopped by after school."

"Yes?" I glance at Momma to see if *she* knows what I

said wrong, but her eyes are closed and she's tapping the tips of her knitting needles against her forehead.

"Really, Francine? A nail boutique? Why not just give her a pouch of marbles and tell her to play in the street?"

"Okay, Mom." Momma opens her eyes and drops the needles in her lap. "What? You want me to work at your club? Is that it?"

"Yes. The pay's excellent and the hours are perfect. Monday through Friday, eight to four. You can still take Ruby to school, and she'll only beat you home by an hour and a half. She might even finish her homework before you're off, and then you'll have the whole night to . . . unwind, or whatever it is you do. I'm friends with the club owner, so if you want the job, it's yours."

This actually sounds pretty good to me, but I can tell right away Momma doesn't agree.

"Thanks," she says, "but I have it under control."

Nana Dottie sighs. "Francine, as we discussed, I'm happy to assume all household expenses, but many others are your responsibility. You need money."

"I have savings."

"They won't last. You need an income."

"Don't take this the wrong way, Mom . . . but no kidding. I've provided for us just fine for thirteen years. I know what I have to do, and I'm doing it."

I open my mouth to talk about anything—school, Ava Grand, Citrus Star—but before I can decide which topic will grab and hold their attention best, the doorbell rings. "Got it!" I exclaim, barely beating Momma to the chance to leave the room. I feel bad, but she *is* the grown-up, and Nana Dottie *is* her mother. As hard as it is, they're going to have to figure this out.

"Quick," Oscar says when I open the door, "what's the Kansas state flower?"

"The sunflower," I say automatically. "Prettiest one in the country."

He's holding both hands behind his back. When I get the answer right, he brings one hand forward.

I gasp. "That's, like, a sunflower *tree*!" It's almost as tall as I am, and its bright yellow blossom is bigger than my head.

"If your grandma doesn't have a vase that'll hold it, let me know. I'll get you one."

My eyes grow wide. "This is for me?"

His smile quickly turns to concern. "You're not allergic, are you?"

"No, not at all." I take the thick stem from him, and then grab it with my other hand. Not only is it as tall as me, it probably weighs as much too. "That was just so nice of you. Thank you."

"Every pretty girl deserves a pretty flower." He leans to the side and peers into the foyer. "Speaking of, is your mom home?"

"*Yes,*" I say, relieved. "And you came just in time."

"Why's that?" He follows me inside. "Order too much Hawaiian pizza?"

"Oscar!" Nana Dottie jumps up from the piano bench and heads toward us before I can answer. "What are you doing here? Did we make a Scrabble date? Did I forget?"

Scrabble. I remember the name from the small toy store in Curly Creek. I also remember wondering how fun a game about letters and words could be. Twister it's not.

"Nope. I just happened to get in a great shipment today and thought I'd share some sunshine with my neighbors." He brings his other hand out from behind his back and holds up two enormous bouquets of flowers.

"Lilies!" Nana Dottie exclaims, taking the white bouquet and lowering her nose to the blossoms. "My favorite."

I watch Oscar step toward Momma, who's still on the couch. She looks like she plans to stay angry for a while, but her face relaxes slightly as he nears, and I catch a quick glimmer of a smile.

"I wasn't sure which was your favorite, Francine," Oscar says, "but these reminded me of you."

I understand instantly why they would. Momma's bouquet is filled with red, pink, hot pink, orange, yellow, and purple daisies. While my sunflower's pretty and Nana Dottie's lilies are elegant, Momma's daisies light up the room.

"Thank you." Momma takes the bouquet and smiles. "They're gorgeous. I didn't know daisies came in so many colors."

"Oscar owns his very own flower shop," Nana Dottie says. "He creates exquisite arrangements for parties, weddings, bar mitzvahs—you name it."

"Wow," I say, trying to imagine what it would be like to work with flowers all day. "That sounds like fun."

"It is," Oscar says. "In fact—"

"That reminds me." Nana Dottie starts across the living room. "I'm hosting a brunch for the girls from the club and would love to discuss some floral options. I'm thinking bright yet subtle, fresh yet classic. Maybe roses? Or tulips? Or . . ."

Nana Dottie's voice fades as she heads down the hall. Apparently, Oscar is supposed to follow her.

"Would you like me to put that in water?" he asks me.

"Please," I say gratefully. My arms ache from holding the sunflower tree. It takes great energy to lift it and pass it to him. "Thank you."

"Francine?" he says.

Momma lifts her face from the daisies. "I think I'd like to hold on to them a little while longer. But thank you so much. That was very kind of you."

It's clear that Momma loves her bouquet. It's also clear by the way Oscar's smile takes up his entire face that this makes him happy.

"He's so nice," I say once he leaves the room.

"He is." The tip of Momma's nose travels from one blossom to the next.

"I wonder how he got to be friends with Nana Dottie. They seem pretty different."

"They do."

I wait several seconds, but Momma doesn't look up. I'd kind of like to talk about what happened before Oscar rang the doorbell, but she seems lost in thought and I don't want to interrupt. I know she'll talk when she's ready, so after a solid two minutes, I return to the desk—and to my laptop.

I've been trying to set up the Internet so I can check my school e-mail account, but I've never set up the Internet before and don't know what I'm doing. I always thought you just popped a computer out of the box, turned it on, and were ready to go. Not so. I managed to plug it in and turn it on, but each time I click on the blue *e* that I know from doing homework at the Curly Creek library is the Internet icon, the screen tells me to check my network connection.

I try again for another ten minutes. I'm so focused on reading and following the instructions that came with the computer, I don't hear myself groan out loud in frustration.

"Want me to try?"

"Yes." I scoot over so Momma can share my chair, and I rattle off all the things I've tried to get it to work.

Momma listens and nods. She glances at the directions and puts them down. She stares at the screen like she's telepathically telling it what to do. And then she holds down the shift key and hits enter.

Not surprisingly, the screen doesn't change.

"Oh well." She shrugs and stands up. "The computer might be a dud. Want to go swimming now?"

"Sure," I say with a sigh. "I'll ask Nana Dottie for help later."

I know Nana Dottie has a computer with Internet access because she's always talking about things she learned online, like country club events, tofu recipes, and weather forecasts. But it doesn't occur to me that asking her for help will somehow bother Momma until the back door quietly slides closed.

I watch through the windows as she takes a tin watering can and fills it with water from the garden hose. She gently places her daisies inside the watering can, carries the makeshift vase to a lounge chair, and sits down. After staring at the pool for several seconds, she leans back and closes her eyes.

Momma looks so pretty sitting by the water with flowers in her lap, I reach for my backpack and take out my camera.

But when I walk closer for a better view, I realize she also looks a little sad. So I change my mind and put the camera away before joining her outside.

9. If I had to rate the next morning on a scale of one to ten, I'd give it a seven and a half.

● Momma was in a good mood during the drive to school, Mr. Fox and I successfully repeated yesterday's best time at the metal detectors, and Ava Grand was too busy planning her Citrus Star performance with her friends to bother me in homeroom. I also paid attention to attendance and learned the name of the nice boy who knows Vivian Vance.

Sam. Which just happens to be one of my all-time favorite boy names ever.

So it was a decent morning. It might've even been a ten if not for the small chocolate stain that I found on my jeans and made bigger by trying to clean it with water and a paper towel, for which I deducted half a point. And the fact that it took place at Sweet Citrus Junior High, which, regardless of everything else, warranted a two-point deduction. Still, all in all, not bad . . . and definitely good enough to keep me from immediately panicking when I see a group of kids gathered around a flat-screen TV in the hallway between fourth and fifth periods.

"What's going on?" I ask a girl at the back of the crowd.

"The Citrus Star lineup is about to be announced." Then, as if just realizing what I said, she looks at me curiously and adds, "Didn't you check your e-mail?"

No, I did not check my e-mail. That would require Internet access, which would require asking Nana Dottie for help, which, as of nine o'clock last night, I wasn't about to do since Momma was still pouting.

"We better be last," another girl declares near the

front of the crowd. "If we're not, I'm totally transferring."

The TV screen explodes into gold sparkles. As the glittery display shifts and spirals across the screen, I scan the crowd. Everyone's staring straight ahead so I can't see faces, but when I spot long, blond hair that looks like it just left a salon hanging over a lavender sundress, I know who's threatening to leave school.

Ava Grand.

"We'll be last." Friend #1 hooks one arm through Ava's arm.

"We have to be." Friend #2 hooks one arm through Ava's other arm.

"If we're not, we're *all* transferring." Friend #3 crosses her arms over her chest, since Ava has no arms left.

The gold glitter thins and trickles to the edges of the screen. A video montage of clips from last year's show starts in the center of the screen. Pockets of cheers, applause, and laughter sound throughout the crowd as kids recognize themselves. I watch closely and take mental notes to review later, when I'm miserably try-ing to figure out what my performance will be. Many kids sing songs I've never heard. Some dance. A few play musical instruments. One girl backflips in place, going faster and faster until she's a blur of black spandex onstage.

I start to relax. The talents are interesting, and most of the kids are really good, but overall, Citrus Star doesn't seem that different from the talent shows back home. After a minute or two, I step back from the crowd. I pull my camera from my backpack. I take a picture of the TV screen, and then quickly hide the camera behind my back. When everyone's too busy admiring themselves to pay attention to me, I take another shot, and another. I'm wondering if I'll be able to put in a new roll of film without anyone noticing when the pockets of cheers and applause swell, then explode.

I cringe at the noise. I haven't heard cheering like this since last November, when Mr. Lou and his wife dressed up as Santa and Mrs. Claus and rode a tractor at the end of the Curly Creek Thanksgiving Day Parade. Kids and adults alike had screamed so loud that the creek, which freezes every winter, cracked.

When I check the TV again, it looks like someone changed the channel. Smoke swirls, lights flash, and a low, deep voice grumbles something about the party getting started. After several seconds, four glittery figures appear, and the crowd—both onscreen and here in the hallway—goes nuts.

Now, Momma and I watch a lot of movies, but we don't care much for regular TV. That might be because we only got one channel in Curly Creek, which was so fuzzy it always looked like local reporters were broadcasting in a blizzard, even in the middle of summer. In any case, Gabby got two hundred crystal-clear channels at her house. (Her dad is a sportsaholic. They got satellite TV so he could watch games played across the country.) And after school one rainy day, we flipped through channels and stopped on one called MTV. We watched a few music videos to see what they were like, and, quickly deciding that if you saw one you saw them all, we turned off the TV and played Monopoly instead.

I hate to admit it, I hate to even *think* it . . . but if any of those videos had been like the performance Ava and her friends gave last year, I don't think we would've been so quick to stop watching.

Because they were good. They were *really* good.

The noise dies down as the video montage ends. The gold glitter swirls across the screen like it's dancing to the funky jazz music playing in the background. Eventually, the glitter forms words: MISS ANITA PRESENTS . . . THE ANNUAL CITRUS STAR LINEUP.

The hallway's practically silent now, and I wonder what the big deal is. If everyone gets a turn, why does it matter who goes first, last, or sometime in between? I'm still clueless as names start drifting across the screen, but I quickly learn from the light squealing that the opening, pre-intermission, post-intermission, and final slots are the ones to get. I also learn that, unfortunately, Ava Grand and company won't be leaving Sweet Citrus Junior High anytime soon, as they'll be closing the show.

The crowd slowly disperses. I make sure my camera's secure in my backpack and then pull out a notebook and a pencil. I've been updating my letter to Gabby every chance I get so she doesn't miss one detail of my new life and will have to write fast to get this update down before the bell rings.

"Uh-oh, Neptune."

I press into the page. The tip of my pencil breaks.

"Here less than a week and already in trouble."

I don't want to look up, but I have no choice. As much as I'd like to pretend Ava Grand doesn't exist, ignoring her isn't worth getting into trouble with anyone else. Plus, I have no idea what I could've done wrong or who I could've upset, and she's clearly the type of person who knows everything about everyone.

"Oh?" I give her the biggest smile I can manage. "Great performance, by the way. Totally professional."

This seems to throw her for a quarter of a second, but then she smirks, flips her hair over one tan shoulder, and nods to the TV screen. My heart lunges in my chest as I follow her nod, and it feels like it might break through when I see what she's referring to.

The screen is no longer gold and sparkly. It's white and blank . . . except for four words pulsating in bold black font.

My face grows hot. My knees shake. I suddenly know exactly how Dorothy feels when she looks to the sky and sees the Wicked Witch of the West flying on her broom and spelling out "Surrender Dorothy" in big, black letters.

"Better hurry," Ava says, and I think I see her nose turn green. "Miss Anita doesn't like to be kept waiting."

The bell rings. Ava and her friends scurry down the hallway, leaving a trail of giggles behind them. I want to move — I *have* to move — but my red Converse are stuck to the linoleum. My eyes are stuck on the screen. I think that the letters will fade or that the TV will simply turn off, but neither happens. I'm working up the courage to look for a power switch when the door behind me swings open and a boy with light brown hair and dark-rimmed glasses darts out.

"Sam?" I turn around, my feet temporarily thawed. "Where are you — ?"

I stop. He's already rounding the corner at the end of the hall, head down, shoulders slumped.

"Hello, Ruby," a cool female voice says. "Come in."

"I can't," I say, barely hearing the words over my pulse drumming in my ears. "I mean, I'd love to stay and chat, of course, but I'm already late for math. Maybe I can stop by after? Or during lunch? Whatever works for you."

A hand touches my shoulder. I look directly into Miss Anita's eyes. Or, more accurately, into her ivory sunglasses, which really make me look into my eyes instead of hers, thanks to their mirrored lenses.

"I'll write you a pass."

"Oh." I try to smile. "Great. Thanks."

I follow her into her office, careful to leave a few feet between us to avoid stepping on the long, light blue skirt that billows behind her. I wonder what she said to Sam that made him run like she was chasing him and if I'm minutes away from doing the same thing. She closes the door gently behind us, and I casually look around for an alternate escape.

"This is a lovely room," I say, partially because a little kindness couldn't hurt in this situation, and also because it's true. "It doesn't feel at all like an office."

"Offices are for principals," Miss Anita says. "I'm a performance director and a dance instructor." She sinks into a soft white chair and crosses her legs. Her shifting skirt sounds like leaves rustling in a breeze.

I'm so impressed by the white furniture, thick white carpet, and multiple vases of purple flowers I almost forget to be nervous. "Whoa. Is that you?"

She doesn't answer, but that doesn't stop me from getting a closer look at the picture hanging on the wall behind her ornate white desk. It's a poster-sized photo of a beautiful ballerina. She wears a sparkly white leotard, a long tulle skirt, and purple satin ballet shoes laced up to the middle of her calves. Her dark hair is twisted into a tight knot at the nape of her neck. She's onstage, and the background is a soft pink blur so that the focus is on her. Her body is turned slightly from the camera, and her head is lowered as if she's sad or deep in thought. Despite the angle of her head, her eyes stare straight ahead. They're not quite blue and not quite purple. They remind me of irises, which are these purplish-blue flowers that popped up around our house each spring. More striking than the color, though, is what they seem to be saying: *Look away. I dare you.*

"You didn't register for Citrus Star."

I tear my eyes away from the ballerina's. As I turn toward Miss Anita, I see other eyes. Dozens of them. They're following me, and I realize they're *my* eyes. Looking down at me from more mirrors than in the entire crazy Hall of Mirrors in the Curly Creek Carnival fun house. There are big mirrors and small mirrors. Round, oval, and square mirrors. Mirrors with metal frames, mirrors with wooden frames. They surround the ballerina picture like a protective glass shield.

"Did I get an e-mail about that?" I finally ask, facing Miss Anita.

"Several."

"I'm sort of having technical difficulties at home. I can't get online."

"You'll need your e-mail if you're going to get through this year."

I think I'll need a lot more than that—namely luck—but somehow doubt Miss Anita is really that concerned about whether I make it through the year.

"You're new, yes?" She leans back.

"Yes, ma'am."

"You realize all students must participate in Citrus Star."

"I've heard that, yes, ma'am."

"Have you also heard that you'll be graded on your performance? And that this grade will live on your permanent transcript from now until the end of time? Potentially paving the way for your success both here and in high school, as well as guiding the trajectory of your entire future?"

A fresh wave of warmth spreads across my cheeks. "No, ma'am."

She doesn't move as she studies me through her sunglasses. "What do you do?"

"I'm sorry?"

She sighs, like I'm trying her patience. "What do you *do*? What's your talent?"

This sounds like a simple question that has a simple

answer. Except, for the life of me, I can't think of one. What *do* I do? Besides watch movies? And hang out with Momma? And count the many reasons why I wish we'd never moved here?

"Do you sing?" Miss Anita prompts. "Act? Dance tap, jazz, or ballet?"

I don't think I've ever felt more like a failure in my entire life. "Not really. I mean, I like to dance for fun . . . but I haven't taken lessons or anything."

Her head lifts then lowers as she sizes me up.

"I take pictures," I say quickly, even though I haven't even developed a single roll of film yet. "I carry my camera with me everywhere."

Her lips press together. I'm about to open my backpack to show her when she stands up—slowly, elegantly, like a blossoming flower. She walks across the room, and I notice she's barefoot. She sinks into the high-backed chair behind her desk, pulls her legs up beneath her, and types something into her computer. She's still wearing her sunglasses, and I wonder how she can see the screen with them on.

"Unfortunately, Ruby, you're the very last student to register. Everyone else has already paired up or formed groups."

"I'm sorry." I step toward the desk, feeling the iris eyes watch me. "I didn't know. It won't happen again."

"That's very nice, but it won't solve this problem, will it?"

In trying to avoid the ballerina and the wall of mirrors, I spot a white grandfather clock in the corner of the room. I'm already ten minutes late to math. If we don't hurry this up, I'll miss class, do poorly on my homework, fail the upcoming test, and potentially flunk school. That has to be a bigger consequence than failing Citrus Star.

"What if—"

"Constellation."

I stand on tiptoe to see over the top of her computer screen. "Excuse me?"

"You'll join the group Constellation. They're excellent, so if you truly have no talent, theirs will make up for it." Her dainty fingers flutter across the keyboard. When she stops typing, the printer next to her computer shoots out a piece of paper. "You're welcome."

"Thank you," I say, even though I'm not sure I'm grateful. I don't have to worry about finding an already formed group to join or, worse, performing solo, but it's obvious Miss Anita helped me only because she found me helpless. Momma always says I can do anything I put my mind to, so this quick dismissal is a first.

The office door opens. I recognize the short man who bursts into the room from Miss Anita's homeroom visit. He's carrying two plastic cups and talking around the paper sack clenched between his teeth. Noticing me, he unclenches his teeth and catches the bag on his forearms.

"The good news is the tuna roll couldn't be fresher if I plucked the fish from the sea myself," he says. "The bad news is they were out of wasabi. But I got you extra soy sauce and had a lengthy conversation with the chef to let him know that this was completely unacceptable. He gave his word that it will never happen again." He pauses. "I didn't realize we were having lunch guests."

"Ruby was just leaving."

They move to the couch and start eating like I'm already gone, so I let myself out. I feel the ballerina's iris eyes on me even after I'm back in the hallway with the door closed. I'm so busy trying to shake the sensation, I don't look at the paper Miss Anita handed me until I'm sitting at my desk in math class.

Thank goodness for small favors. Because if I hadn't already been sitting down I would've fallen over.

According to the printout, there are four members in Constellation besides me.

Hilary Smith. Megan Hanley. Stephanie Zilco.

And Ava Grand.

10.

"Don't do it, Dorothy. Stay home. Just stay home, where everyone loves you and nothing will hurt you."

She doesn't listen. I shake my head and shove another handful of popcorn in my mouth. What's so great over the rainbow? What's so wrong *under* the rainbow? I think if you can see it, stand below it, and appreciate its pretty colors from afar, that should be enough. Unfortunately, Dorothy is going to learn this the hard way.

I pause the movie, then pick up the phone and dial Gabby's number. It's still busy. It's been busy for twenty minutes, and I try not to think about what this must mean: Gabby has a new best friend. One she talks to for hours every night even though they spent all day together at school, just like we used to. I've been gone less than a month, and I've already been replaced.

I un-pause the movie and watch Dorothy visit the fortune-teller. He guesses that she's running away because she feels unappreciated, but he convinces her to return home.

"Listen to him, Dorothy," I urge, cramming another handful of popcorn in my mouth.

She does, but the universe decides to teach her a lesson anyway. As the tornado nears, their farmhouse shakes. Miss Almira Gulch, the Wicked Witch of Kansas who threatens to get Dorothy and her little dog, too, flies past a window on her bike.

Miss Almira makes me think of Miss Anita. Miss Anita makes me think of Citrus Star. Citrus Star makes me think of Constellation. Constellation makes me think of Ava Grand. And all that thinking makes me pick up the phone and dial Gabby's number again.

"Hello?"

I haven't even punched in the last number when I hear a voice. Maybe Nana Dottie's phone is so high tech it remembers your calling patterns and does the work for you. "Mrs. Kibben?" I say, bringing the receiver to my ear. "Hi! It's Ruby."

"Ruby, I'm on the phone."

I pause. That's pretty obvious.

"I'll be off in a bit. Would you mind calling your friend later?"

My friend?

"Oh, and your mother asked me to tell you that she's bringing home Chinese food for dinner. Though how they can call that fried nonsense 'food' is beyond me."

Ah. It's not Mrs. Kibben after all. The phone must've already been in use when I picked it up. "Sorry, Nana Dottie," I say, and hang up.

I eat popcorn and watch Dorothy meet the Munchkins. After fifteen minutes, I pause the movie and try the phone again. This time I listen first instead of automatically pushing buttons. When I hear Nana Dottie telling someone about a recent tennis match, I gently hang up.

I do this three more times over the course of an hour. By the third try, Dorothy has already picked up the Scarecrow, the Tin Man, and the Cowardly Lion, and is well on her way to Oz. I begin to worry that I won't get to talk to Gabby at all tonight, since it's Thursday and she'll be leaving for Curly Creek Cosmic Bowling Night soon. And if I don't talk to her tonight, I probably won't talk to her again until Monday, since Friday through Sunday nights are always jam-packed with drive-in movies, board-game parties, and sleepovers.

Suddenly, I feel quite jealous of Dorothy. She may be far from home and have no idea where she's going, but at least her friends are with her as she tries to find her way.

"I'm off the phone, Ruby."

I look up. Nana Dottie's standing in the family room doorway. She starts to smile but stops after scanning the room.

"What on earth happened in here?"

I sit up on the couch, sending granola bar wrappers fluttering to the floor. At first I don't know what she's talking about, but then I realize she probably hasn't been in this room in a while, since she never watches TV.

"Momma's using this as a temporary work space," I say.

"'Work space' implies that work is being done. All I see here are mountains of yarn, knitting needles tossed about like confetti, and garbage."

I look around. Nana Dottie's eyes don't lie. "She says if a room's too neat, her creativity can't breathe," I explain.

Nana Dottie picks up an open bag of potato chips from the coffee table. She holds one corner of the bag between her thumb and forefinger, lowers her head, and sniffs. "Forget creativity." She reels back and drops the bag on the table. "What about you? How can *you* breathe when this place smells like McDonald's?"

Mmm. McDonald's. Maybe Momma will change her mind and get Happy Meals instead of egg rolls for dinner.

I shrug. "I'm fine."

Apparently, something in my voice makes Nana Dottie think otherwise. She seems to forget the mess as she steps into the room. She glances at the TV, on which Dorothy and her friends are waking up in the beautiful poppy field, and then pushes aside a pile of orange yarn on the couch before sitting down.

I think she's going to say something—most likely something disapproving about Momma—but she doesn't. She simply sits back and watches the movie.

"I love this part," she says when Dorothy and her friends are whisked away for makeovers after reaching the Emerald City.

"You've seen *The Wizard of Oz*?"

She looks at me, surprised that I'm surprised. "Well, of course I have. Who hasn't? It's only the greatest movie of all time."

She looks at the TV again, and I smile. *I* think *The Wizard of Oz* is the greatest movie of all time, but until she said so, I never would've thought Nana Dottie liked it too. Her DVD collection consists of documentaries about classical composers and classical music concerts. *The Wizard of Oz* seems too . . . silly . . . for someone so reserved and refined.

"That reminds me," she says after the Tin Man emerges from his buff-and-polish looking shiny and new, "we should probably get you a cell phone."

She says this so casually I almost nod before fully processing the suggestion.

"We'll get you something simple and just add you to my plan."

She's still looking at the TV, like the idea of buying me a cell phone is no big deal. Even though it's a *huge* deal—especially since Momma hates cell phones. She thinks they're enormous wastes of time and money and believes they drive people apart instead of bringing them together. I know this. Nana Dottie knows this. So why's she suggesting I get one when Momma's not even here to discuss it?

"It's very nice of you to offer," I say just as casually, "but I don't know if I really need a cell phone."

"Don't you talk to your best friend every night?"

"Yes, ma'am, but—"

"And didn't we just have a situation wherein we both wanted to use the phone at the same time?"

"Yes, ma'am, but—"

"So we'll get you your own. It'll be convenient and economically efficient. My plan includes free long distance and unlimited nights and weekends. And I already have a ton of rollover minutes I'll have moved to your account."

I don't understand half of what she's saying but know I have to change her mind before it becomes permanently decided. "But most kids my age don't have cell phones."

Nana Dottie looks at me and lifts one eyebrow. "That might be true in Curly Creek. But you're in Coconut Grove now."

She's right. At Sweet Citrus, as soon as the bell rings after eighth period, kids whip out their cell phones to call their parents, nannies, babysitters, or personal assistants and remind them where they need to go at what time and when they need to be picked up. They're so fast, so businesslike, I've wondered if the only reason kids in Curly Creek *don't* have cell phones is because they're just not in that big of a rush to get anywhere. And since I don't ever have anywhere to be, let alone anywhere I have to be quickly, it seems pretty unnecessary.

Although, I have to admit . . . it would be nice to call Gabby whenever I want without worrying about tying up Nana Dottie's line.

"Would you look at that?" Nana Dottie smiles at the TV when Dorothy reunites with her friends after their makeovers. "She's as pretty as a picture."

Pretty as a picture. I look at Dorothy but see the ballerina with the iris eyes. My mind replays snippets of my conversation with Miss Anita. A cell phone might be fun, but considering Miss Anita's not-so-friendly sort-of advice, another technological advancement is essential.

"Nana Dottie," I say timidly, "what do you know about the Internet?"

"Enough to teach a class of thirty retirees at the Coconut Grove Public Library. By the time I'm done with them, they're surfing like pros."

"Do you know how to hook it up on a new computer?"

She looks at me, eyes wide. "You're not . . . ? Your mother didn't . . . ?"

I shake my head, unable to admit our technological failings out loud. It's embarrassing, and I also don't want Momma to think I ratted her out by answering Nana Dottie's second incomplete question.

"Where's your laptop?"

"In the living room."

The words are barely out of my mouth when she jumps up. I quickly gather the empty granola bar wrappers, stuff them in the popcorn bowl, and stop the movie. When I reach the living room, Nana Dottie already has the laptop open and is typing away.

"I'm really sorry," I say, standing behind the desk chair and peering over her shoulder. "I know I should know how to do this, but we just didn't use the computer much back home. I mean, back in Curly Creek." I hope she doesn't see my reflection wince in the computer screen.

"Ruby." She swivels in the chair to face me. I expect her to look angry, or at the very least, annoyed. But she doesn't. If anything, she looks sad. "You never have to apologize for not knowing what you haven't been taught."

I look down at my red Converse. I'm pretty sure she's not just referring to the Internet, and wish I had at least some idea of what else I don't know.

"Now, why don't you go get a piece of paper and a pencil? I'll give you a lesson, and then you'll always be able to get online, no matter where you are." She turns back to the computer as I hurry toward my backpack. "And I love questions, so make sure you ask a lot!"

After our thirty-minute lesson, it's clear that Coconut Grove's technologically challenged retirees are in extremely good hands. Nana Dottie teaches me everything there is to know about the Internet and then some. I learn which cord to plug in where, what a network is and how to configure one, why I need a firewall to block harmful viruses, and how to search for healthy vegetarian recipes. I'm nervous at first, but Nana Dottie's very patient. And she wasn't lying when she said she loves questions. Each time I ask one, she listens thoughtfully and answers in such a way that I never feel silly. If I don't get it right away, she tries explaining it differently until I do.

"How did you learn all this?" I ask in awe when we're done.

Smiling, she removes a small square cloth from the desk and wipes the spotless laptop screen. "Papa Harry loved computers like I love crosswords. To him, they were great, challenging puzzles. He taught me the basics of e-mail and search engines, and then when he got sick and couldn't tinker like he used to, I picked up a lot by reading him computer books and magazines."

I pause. This is the first time Nana Dottie's mentioned Papa Harry since the day I asked about the yellow convertible in the garage. This is also the first time since we've been here that she's referred to what happened to him. And since what happened to him and how that affected her were the reasons we moved here, I don't know how to respond.

Do I say I'm sorry? Ask how she's feeling? Ask if she misses him, or if there's anything I can do? The moment suddenly feels too big, too important for me to handle on my own, and I find myself listening for Momma's car growling in the driveway.

"Ready for more?" she asks after several seconds.

"More?"

"Don't you need to know how to access your school e-mail?"

"Oh. Yes, I definitely do."

I'm relieved and disappointed that Nana Dottie doesn't offer more about Papa Harry and wonder if I should ask about him anyway, just to let her know I care. Before I can decide, she turns back to the computer and starts typing. Knowing the conversation is done for now, I find the e-mail instructions in the Sweet Citrus information packet on the desk.

"I'll bookmark the link so all you have to do is click on it and then enter your username and password." Nana Dottie barely glances at the instructions I've spent hours trying to decipher. "And here you go."

I watch the screen fill with unread e-mails. When my in-box hits fifty, I'm sure each new note will be the last, but then another pops up. And another, and another. "Those are all for me?" I ask, thinking there must be a mistake. The most e-mails I ever had in my Curly Creek library account was ten, and that was only when Gabby sent me jokes from a funny new website she discovered.

"Don't worry, they look fairly standard. Lunch menus, fund-raiser announcements, sports schedules . . . and about a hundred regarding Citrus Star."

"A *hundred*?" My stomach flip-flops as I lean forward for a better look.

"Maybe more." Nana Dottie scrolls down so I can see what she means. "Have you decided which talent to astound the audience with yet?"

I look at her. "You know about Citrus Star?"

"Of course. It's quite an affair. Papa Harry and I went every year."

"Really? Papa Harry's grandchildren went to Sweet Citrus?"

"He didn't have grandchildren—besides you, of

course. The show's open to the community, so we always went with some of our friends. It's so popular they hold it at the Coconut Grove Theater downtown instead of in the junior high auditorium. And even in that large space it's standing room only."

My head spins with this new information. "How many people does the Coconut Grove Theater hold?"

"There are six hundred seats, and another fifty people can stand in the back. There's also an overflow room that shows the performances on an enormous television. That room holds a hundred people. And they usually set up an outdoor viewing area around a drive-in movie screen for especially large productions—like Citrus Star."

My legs wobble beneath me. I grab the desk for support. "How many people can fit in the outdoor viewing area?"

Nana Dottie tilts her head as she thinks about this. "Two hundred? Two-fifty?" She shrugs. "It's always hard to tell with all those reporters and news crews milling about."

Thankfully, the phone rings then and she gets up to answer it. I drop into the desk chair and stare at the computer screen without seeing it. I'm pretty good at math, so it doesn't take long to add up the numbers.

A thousand people. Plus reporters and news crews whose coverage could reach thousands more. Which means not only am I weeks away from looking like an idiot in front of my classmates and their families, I'm weeks away from looking like an idiot in front of the entire state of Florida.

If only Coconut Grove had a magical field of poppies, I'd lie down for a nice long nap and not wake up until Citrus Star's curtain call.

11. The auditorium at Sweet Citrus Junior High is ten times bigger than the one at Curly Creek Junior High. It's ten times fancier too. Each blue velvet seat is so wide it could comfortably fit two people instead of one. The dark wood floor is so shiny you can look at your feet and check your hair at the same time. The ivory walls are framed by an intricate floral trim made of dark wood that matches the floor. Drapes of blue satin hang from the ceiling like the full sails of a dozen boats. And its most striking feature is the beautiful blue velvet curtain that spans the full length of the stage.

Compared to the Curly Creek Junior High auditorium, with its ripped vinyl seats, peeling walls, and patched canvas curtain, the Sweet Citrus Junior High auditorium might as well be on Broadway. (I haven't been to Broadway, of course, but from what I've heard and read, the Sweet Citrus auditorium would fit in perfectly.)

"Pick it up, Megan!"

I jump. You'd think Ava Grand would want to save her voice, but she keeps bellowing like a foghorn.

"Did someone stomp through a puddle of wet cement this morning? An *elephant* is lighter on its feet."

My heart races as if this insult is directed at me, though I know it can't be. I'm still standing against the back wall, where I've been standing for twenty minutes. Ava doesn't know I'm here, and I'm just waiting for the right time to tell her.

Onstage, Megan, Stephanie, and Hilary run through what I assume is supposed to be a dance routine but what looks more like a futuristic version of the Hokey Pokey. They're in a circle, taking turns popping various body parts in the circle's center, but their movements are rigid, awkward. They look like robots in black leotards and fuzzy pink leg warmers.

"Enough!" Ava calls out over the thumping music. "*Enough*! You're giving me a migraine. I need a break."

The stage lights dim and the overhead lights come on. The dancing robots sit down, their legs dangling over the edge of the stage. I'm tempted to dash into the hallway before anyone notices me but know the longer I wait, the worse it'll be. And now might be my only chance—this is the first break they've taken, and from what I've seen of Ava's directing so far, it might be the last.

Besides, how bad can it be? It's not like I *asked* to be in their group. If they have a problem, they can take it up with Miss Anita.

I take a deep breath and slowly start down the aisle. I'm halfway down when the song the robots were dancing to ends and the auditorium falls silent. The only noises are the soft whooshing of a feathered fan Ava waves frantically in front of her face . . . and the loud clomping of my Converse.

"This is a closed rehearsal!" Ava shouts without turning around.

I stop. I'd run out, except I've been spotted. Two of the dancing robots see me and hop off the stage to alert their leader. The third, who I know is Megan from her unfortunate missteps and Ava's scolding, watches me curiously.

"Pluto? What do you think you're doing?" Ava storms up the aisle, blond hair flying behind her. "Are you lost in orbit?"

"Pluto's not a planet," I say.

She stands two feet away from me and puts her hands on her hips. Behind her, the two robots that alerted her to my presence take turns waving the feather fan at the back of her head. "Excuse me?"

"It *was* a planet, but now it's not. It was downgraded to nonplanet status a while ago." I realize I'm venturing into dangerous territory, but if all I've got on Ava Grand is some silly astronomy trivia, I'll use it while I can.

She starts to fire back, but then adjusts her aim when Megan half snorts, half laughs onstage. "Something funny, Dumbo?" she shoots over her shoulder.

"That was a sneeze." Megan sniffs. "Sorry."

Ava turns back to me. "The auditorium's ours until four o'clock."

"I know." Any triumph I just felt vanishes. Fear returns. What was I thinking, trying to one-up Ava Grand? No one could ever one-up her. She's un-one-uppable.

She closes her eyes and rubs her temples. "I know you're new, so I'm going to let this little security breach slide."

"Security breach?" I glance behind me. The door wasn't locked. Did I miss the bodyguards?

"Stephanie," Ava says with a sigh, sounding the way Miss Anita did when I was wearing her patience.

"Our rehearsals are top secret," one of the robots says. Up close I can see that, like Ava, she's quite pretty.

She has chin-length brown hair, green eyes, and freckles that cluster together when she smiles—which she does now, probably because she's excited to be the chosen one that gets to explain the breach to me.

"*Top*, top secret," the other robot says. By process of elimination, this one, with the black curly hair, brown eyes, and dimples, is Hilary. "You don't want to know what happened to the last girl who tried to copy our act."

She's right. I don't. Because given the way they all exchange smug smirks and giggles, that poor girl is probably still doing time for the crime—if she hasn't already changed her name and fled the country.

"I'm not here to spy," I say. "I'm here to join you."

This seems to amuse them even more. "I'm sorry?" Ava says, her wide smile revealing perfectly white, perfectly straight teeth that would make my orthodontist back home weep with joy. "What did you just say?"

I know repeating myself will only fuel their laughter, so I reach into my jeans pocket and pull out a folded piece of paper.

"Hilary." Ava eyes the paper like it's covered in spiders as I hold it toward her.

Hilary dutifully takes the note. Stephanie tries not to look disappointed that she wasn't given this important assignment.

"Dear Ruby," Hilary reads, "here's Constellation's rehearsal schedule."

Ava's chin drops.

"You're already behind," Hilary continues nervously, "so if you have plans that conflict with any of these times, cancel them. Pay attention. Work hard. Cry if you have to. Give up sleep if you must. Once you hear the audience roar, it will all be worth it. Regards, Miss Anita."

"Let me see that." Ava snatches the note from Hilary.

"It's on her ballet e-stationery," Hilary says. "It's really from—"

Ava holds up one hand for silence. Her blue eyes travel from the top of the page to the bottom, and then back again. She reads it five times before shaking her head. "She just dumps the new girl on me without even *asking*? Is she crazy? Does she know who I am? Does she know who my father is?"

She crumples the note in her fist and spins on one heel. Hilary and Stephanie shoot each other worried looks before running after her. When they reach their big leather purses sitting in the front row, Ava grabs hers and yanks out a cell phone. Hilary tries to fan Ava as she dials, but Ava shoves her arm away.

I stand where they left me, not sure what to do. If I stay, Ava and the fuzzy-legged robots will likely tie me up in blue velvet and leave me on the catwalk above the stage. If I leave, I'm definitely on my own for Citrus Star. I can't believe I don't know which option's worse . . . but I don't.

"Hydrating! Be right back!"

I look up from my Converse to see Megan waving an empty bottle overhead and running toward me. Despite Ava's earlier accusation, Megan can move—and fast.

"Thirsty?" she whispers as she passes me without slowing down.

Is that an invitation? A command? What if Ava

summons me and I'm not here? Won't that make her angrier?

"I will *not* blow this opportunity over some lost little new girl who dresses like a boy and hardly speaks! Constellation has a reputation to uphold, and—"

I'm through the auditorium doors before Ava can finish shouting into the phone about the many ways in which I'm not worthy of sharing her stage.

"Pretty hot in there, huh?" Megan's standing by a water fountain, refilling her bottle.

"It's hot everywhere here." I sit on a bench in the middle of the lobby. After a few seconds, Megan joins me.

"She sounds worse than she is."

"You mean her bark's worse than her bite?"

She tilts her head and seems to think about this. "Yes. Good one, Ruby!"

I'd explain that the expression's not mine to take credit for but am thrown by the fact that she knows my name. And that she used it instead of calling me a planet—or a nonplanet, as the case may be.

"You know how some kids love Christmas? Like,

really love it? So much so that every year, they count down the months, weeks, days, hours, minutes, and seconds until December twenty-fifth? Because they're never as happy as they are on Christmas morning, when they open presents and hang out with their families and eat huge breakfasts?"

I know the kids Megan means. I'm one of them. I don't share this, though. She seems nice enough . . . but what if her niceness is just an act? Another way to get information they can use to embarrass me later?

"Citrus Star is Ava's Christmas," she continues before I can decide. "She looks forward to it all year, every year. As soon as it's over, she starts researching and preparing for the next one. Last year, she signed us up for a modern dance class at six in the morning the day after Citrus Star. I didn't know whether to hate her or admire her."

"Which did you finally choose?"

"Admiration, of course." Her eyes catch mine as she takes a long gulp of water. "Though I will never, *ever* show anyone my diary entry from that day."

Despite my wariness, I smile.

"For Ava, Citrus Star is a warm-up for the main event. She wants to be a Hollywood triple threat and act, sing, and dance her way to international superfame." She shrugs. "Just like most kids at Sweet Citrus."

"Most kids here want to grow up to be famous?"

"Some of them already are, at least on a smaller scale. Ava's been doing catalog and commercial work since she was three years old and has been trying to get an agent for about as long."

Megan gulps more water, and I think about what she's just shared. Back home, kids dreamed of being doctors, teachers, and veterinarians. I personally dreamed of owning a restaurant—someplace fun and relaxed where everyone automatically gathered after baseball games and other events. We wanted to be part of and contribute to a close-knit community. Achieving international superfame—or even local semifame—never crossed my mind.

"I'm *starving*," Megan declares suddenly, crossing one arm over her stomach. "We started our low-carb Citrus Star diet this week, and my body's still mad at me. What I wouldn't give for some potato chips or chocolate."

"How about both?" I lift my backpack into my lap, unzip it, and open my lunch box without taking it from the bag. I didn't get to eat lunch today, since I never found an empty table and was forced to circle the cafeteria all period. "Momma's a firm believer in the salty-sweet food combo."

She gasps as I hold up the plastic snack bags. "Me too!"

I smile again. She didn't even seem to notice that I just called my mom "Momma." Maybe her niceness is genuine, after all.

"*You*, Ruby Lee, are a lifesaver." She grins and reaches one hand into each bag. "Thanks."

"Sure," I say, even though I want to thank her, too. If I'm right about her sincerity, then she's not the only one who's just been saved.

"Megan Marie Hanley!" Ava shrieks from inside the auditorium. "Wherever you are, you better be prying the cement from your feet!"

"Think that's my cue?" Megan asks me, pretending to be serious.

I giggle. As she hops up and heads for the auditorium door, I stuff the potato chips and chocolate back into my lunch box.

"By the way?" She stops in front of the door and looks at me. "I've seen *Mamma Mia!* eleven times. 'Take a Chance on Me' is my favorite song."

My hands freeze on the ABBA lunch box still inside my backpack. I've kept it hidden since that first day at the metal detectors to avoid further embarrassment . . . but *Mamma Mia!* is a musical filled with ABBA songs. Is it possible Megan saw my lunch box and actually *liked* it?

She disappears into the auditorium before I can ask. I finish zipping up my backpack and hurry inside. By the time the door closes behind me, she's already joining Hilary and Stephanie onstage.

"We're taking the routine from the top," Ava shouts over the weird thumping music that's starting again. "Pluto—which, as a non-planet, is an even better nickname than I thought—will sit and watch until this situation is resolved. She absolutely cannot participate, and I refuse to lose another precious minute of rehearsal time."

I'm still so excited by what just happened in the lobby that Ava's latest insult doesn't even sting. I happily drop into a velvet seat in the back row. As they practice, I think about all the questions I'll ask Megan as soon as we're alone again.

"*Clearly,*" Ava yells several minutes later, "concrete feet are contagious. Who knew?"

My stomach flip-flops sympathetically as Hilary, Stephanie, and Megan stop dancing. They bend over, rest their hands on the tops of their thighs, and catch their breath. They're still recovering from the exertion when the music changes and Ava stomps up the stage steps.

"Watch and learn, ladies." Ava strides to center stage. She's wearing a long white robe and removes it to reveal a silver leotard; silver leg warmers; and a sheer, shimmery skirt that falls to her knees. She holds out the robe, and Hilary scampers across the stage to take it. Ava points to the front row, and the three girls dash down the steps and sit down. "Lights!"

The room grows dark except for the round spotlight shining on Ava. As the funky instrumental intro picks up, she places one foot in front of the other and lowers her head. She stands perfectly still, glittering from head to toe.

I hold my breath. She hasn't even done anything, and she already looks like a star.

Still looking down, she lifts one arm, then the other. Her movements are slow, dramatic. The music builds, its beats coming louder and faster. Her eyes are closed as she starts to lift her head, one vertebra at a time. The music's so loud now, the blue velvet seat vibrates beneath me. I'm about to cover my ears against the thunderous drumming when the scream of an electric guitar drowns it out.

Ava's eyes snap open. The spotlight glows a brilliant white.

The sudden light is blinding, and I have to turn away. I try looking again when I hear some sort of commotion taking place onstage, but all I see are a million tiny white spots dancing in front of my eyes. By the time they fade, the spotlight's gone and the overhead lights are on.

"Are you *insane*?" Ava howls. She's still onstage and is now flanked by Hilary and Stephanie, who help her back into her robe. She's trembling like she's just been struck by lightning. "What if my retinas are burned? What if I need surgery? What if I go blind? Do you have *any* idea what you could've just done?"

She fires this attack out at the auditorium, and since I'm the only one here, I'm worried she thinks I somehow messed with the spotlight to get back at her. But then I hear a noise overhead, and I realize she's not just firing this attack *out*—she's firing it *up*. At the lighting booth.

"Sorry about that," a male voice calls out, not sounding particularly sorry at all. "Technical difficulty. It won't happen again."

Protected by shadows, I sit back in my seat and smile. This rehearsal just keeps getting better and better. I haven't heard that voice much, but I'd still know it anywhere.

Because it belongs to Sam.

12.

"Are you sure I look okay?"

"No," I say. "I'm sure you look great."

Momma shoots me a quick smile and turns back to the ice-cream-shop window that's serving as a full-length mirror. Then she straightens her shirt and pats her hair. She leans toward the window, puckers up, and checks her lipstick.

"They think so too."

Momma laughs when she sees the ice-cream scoopers puckering back. She blows an exaggerated kiss, which makes them laugh, and then takes my hand and continues walking.

This exchange is a good sign. We've been walking for an hour. Momma said she needed to get the lay of the land, with "the land" being the HauteCoco shopping center, but this is our fifth lap. We're no longer exploring— we're stalling. If we stall much longer, it'll be too late to do what we came to do. But since she joked with the ice-cream scoopers instead of avoiding them, the way she had with every HauteCoco employee and customer we'd encountered up until now, she must be feeling more relaxed. Which must mean she's almost ready.

"How about this one?" I ask as we near Gifts of the Grove. "It looks like Mr. Lou's store."

Momma slows down slightly to peek into the open doorway. "Too fancy."

We keep walking. Gifts of the Grove, which sells Florida T-shirts, mugs, and keychains as well as other non-Florida fare like candles, figurines, and assorted knickknacks, is definitely the *least* fancy of all the HauteCoco stores. But I don't say this out loud.

Momma's squeezing my hand like hers might fall off if she lets go, even though it's about a thousand degrees out and our palms are slippery with sweat.

"This one looks nice," I say a few stores later. I understand her nervousness, but I also know she'll only feel worse if we leave without accomplishing anything.

"Too stuffy."

I can't argue that. The suits and ties inside Aspire Menswear do look nice, but the atmosphere's a bit stiff for Momma's taste; it's very quiet, and the store's one employee is an older man in a three-piece suit who stands near the doorway and stares at a potted fern. It's a far cry from the Curly Creek Nail Boutique, which was always bustling with activity and filled with happy, laughing customers.

"This one looks promising," I say in front of Board-walk. A quick check inside shows three employees help-ing three teenagers shop for bikinis.

Momma looks in and shakes her head. "Too young."

We keep walking, and I stop making suggestions. Maybe Momma's just not ready for this. And if she's not, that's totally fine. There's no reason to rush. Nana Dottie will just have to understand that we're still settling and that certain things will fall into place when the time's right.

A few minutes later, we pass the ice-cream shop and head into lap seven. My feet hurt. My camera, which hangs around my neck, feels like it weighs a hundred pounds. And I'm starting to get hungry. I don't want to encourage stalling, but I could really go for a snack right now. Preferably something cold in an air-conditioned restaurant. I'm about to ask if we can take a break when Momma stops short.

"This one," she says, facing a small store with a light green awning. "This one's perfect."

I step toward the window for a better look. The racks and shelves inside are filled with women's clothing and accessories, and a young woman sits behind the counter, reading a book. Two customers try on straw hats in front of a mirror. I'm not sure what makes this store better than any of the others, but if Momma likes it, that's all that matters.

"Perfect," I agree.

Still holding my hand, she gently tugs me away from the window. When we're out of sight of the people inside, she releases my hand and fans her face with her own.

"You're going to be great," I say before nerves can change her mind. "They're going to love you. They'll probably even ask you to start today and pay you a thousand dollars an hour."

"I don't know." She opens her purse and pulls out a packet of tissues. "The only job I've ever had was at the Curly Creek Nail Boutique. What if everything's different here?"

I think we learned the answer to that question weeks ago, but know now's not the time to say so. "Then you'll learn. No big deal."

She blots her face with a tissue, then runs a brush through her hair and puts on a fresh coat of pink lipstick. She unbuttons and rebuttons her jacket and flicks an imaginary piece of lint from her skirt. She takes another tissue and bends down to wipe the imaginary dust from her heels.

"Momma," I say.

She looks up.

"You know how you always tell me I can do any-thing in the world I set my mind to?"

"Sure do. And you can."

I hold out my hand for the tissue. "So can you."

For a second I think she might cry—which would make her mascara run, which would require a trip to the restroom, which would only prolong the stalling—but then she gives me the tissue and kisses the top of my head. "Thank you, baby girl."

She takes a deep breath and squares her shoulders. As she heads for the store, I think she's never looked more beautiful. She's wearing a black suit and black high heels, which she bought just for the occasion, and a pearl necklace she'd found at Curly Creek Junk 'n' Treasures years ago. She looks so professional, any store would be crazy not to hire her on the spot. Not wanting to miss this store's offer, I hurry after her and stand behind a palm tree near the entrance. I also take three pictures of Momma inside the store, since I know she'll want to remember the exact moment her new career took off.

"Hi there." Momma's voice is louder than normal, but not so loud that anyone would automatically know how nervous she is.

"Hello." The woman sitting at the counter looks up from her book and smiles. "Welcome to EcoChic."

EcoChic. That makes sense. I learned all about being eco-friendly last year, when Curly Creek started its first-ever recycling program. To get our attention during a school-wide presentation about the importance of reusing what we can, Principal Perkins stood onstage in an old brown potato sack he found in Farmer Cott's barn. ("As durable as a pair of jeans—and good for the environment too!" he'd declared.) The shirts, skirts, and dresses inside EcoChic are all various shades of tan and seem to be made of light, natural material. They have more shape than a potato sack, but besides that, they look like they could've been found in Farmer Cott's barn too.

"I'm Laurel," the saleswoman says. "May I help you find something?"

"Why, yes," Momma says. "Yes, you can."

Don't say it, I think, watching her approach the counter. *Please don't say it.*

"You can help me find a job!"

I close my eyes. Of course she said it. Momma jokes a lot under normal circumstances, but even more so when she's nervous. I can only hope Laurel has a good sense of humor.

"I'm Francine Lee," Momma says. I open my eyes to see her extend one hand. "Formerly of Curly Creek, Kansas, currently of Coconut Grove. It's a pleasure."

"It's very nice to meet you." Laurel shakes Momma's hand. "But I'm afraid we're not hiring right now."

My heart sinks.

"Well, I'm in no rush," Momma says, and I can tell she's trying not to sound disappointed. "Maybe I could fill out an application? And you can just give me a buzz when something opens up?"

"We don't have applications. Clementine, the owner, doesn't believe in them."

"How about a résumé?" Momma rummages through

her tote bag. "I haven't worked in very many places, but I've done lots of jobs. I can answer phones, and chat up customers, and up-sell a manicure into a manicure, pedicure, and full-body massage."

I understand what Momma's trying to say—that she can charm customers into buying what they didn't think they wanted—but don't blame Laurel for looking confused.

"I also have a list of references. Please feel free to fire away. These people have known me my entire life and can tell you anything you want to know—including how I celebrated my fifth birthday, what I wore to my high school prom, and how I take my coffee."

Laurel moves aside a small white cup as Momma places a folder on the counter. I frown when I see a teabag tag hanging down the side of the cup. Laurel drinks tea, not coffee. She probably drinks it plain too, and not loaded up with cream and sugar.

"That's very nice," Laurel says as Momma slides papers toward her, "and I'm happy to take a look. But you should know that we've had the same staff for eight years. We're not likely to hire anyone anytime soon."

I duck behind the palm tree as the two women who'd been trying on straw hats leave the store.

"Does she have a hearing problem?" one woman asks the other once they're outside. "How many times does she have to hear 'no' before giving up?"

"And what about that outfit?" the other woman clucks. "All black, from head to toe. She clearly doesn't know where she is. I almost feel sorry for her."

I bite my lip to keep from jumping to Momma's defense. I normally wouldn't hesitate but don't want to cause a stir right now, when Momma's still talking to Laurel.

I peer out from behind the tree again to see Laurel on the phone and Momma leaning against the counter, waiting to continue their conversation. I hate that the pair of gossipy snobs makes me look at Momma's outfit again . . . but they do. And I would never say so out loud, but unfortunately, I see their point. Compared to Laurel's ivory linen dress and all the neutral-colored clothes in the store, Momma's black suit does look a bit out of place.

She catches my eye and winks. I smile.

She still looks beautiful. And EcoChic would still be lucky to have her.

"Here's the thing," Momma says when Laurel's off the phone. She sounds calmer, more like herself. "I understand what you're telling me, but *you* should know that I'll do anything. I'm a fast learner, and I'll do whatever needs to be done. I'll answer phones, clean, sell, ship, organize, stock—whatever. Your store's different from all the other stores here. It's beautiful, but it also has a purpose beyond selling clothes and accessories. In many ways, it reminds me of home. I would be honored—and grateful—to be a member of the EcoChic family."

I watch Laurel's face soften. Just like the gossips, she didn't give Momma enough credit.

"I'll tell you what," Laurel says. "Why don't you wait here, and I'll go get Clementine? You can tell her everything you just told me. She might not give you a different answer, but I think it's worth a try."

"That would be wonderful," Momma says. "Thank you."

I give her a quick thumbs-up when she turns to me and grins. Laurel returns to the counter a moment later. An older woman with short white-blond hair is with her. Just as Laurel is about to make introductions, the outdoor music switches from a soft piano ballad to a loud, jumpy pop song. I can barely hear the voices inside the store now, so I dash from my palm tree and squat behind a flowering shrub a few inches closer to the entrance. Unfortunately, the shrub hides an in-ground speaker, and the music's so loud here I can't hear anything but thumping bass and squeaky lyrics. I'm considering dropping to the ground and rolling past the entrance to try a bush on the other side when Momma comes flying out.

I jump up from my squat. "What happened? Where are you—"

"Home, Ruby Lee," she calls back without turning around. "We're going home."

My heart flits in my chest. Does she mean home, home? Kansas, home?

"By the way, love your bag! Where'd you get it?"

I turn to see the woman with short white-blond hair standing in the EcoChic doorway. Laurel stands behind her. They're both watching Momma, who's now kicking off her heels in the middle of the courtyard so she can move faster. The only bag she carries is the one she finished knitting last night.

"She made it," I say.

Clementine looks at me, surprised.

"She makes lots of things," I add. "She's very talented. You would've found that out if you gave her a chance."

She opens her mouth to say something, but I hurry after Momma before she can. By the time I reach the car three blocks over, Momma's already taken off her jacket and wiggled out of her panty hose. I want to ask if she's okay but know there's really no point. Because she's clearly *not* okay. And she definitely doesn't feel like talking. As soon as we get in the car she cranks up the *Grease* soundtrack and punches the gas without a word.

For a while, I think we really might be going back

to Kansas. We drive for over an hour, taking roads and turns I don't recognize. I monitor Momma's emotional state by watching her fingers curl around the steering wheel. They start out white, then slowly turn pink, then tan. I wait until she's calm enough to drive with one tan hand before speaking.

"Momma?" I say gently. "If we're going home, do you think we should maybe stop by Nana Dottie's first? To get our stuff and say good-bye?"

The car slows suddenly, like someone just tickled under Momma's right knee and made her foot hop off the gas pedal.

"Or we could just keep going," I say quickly. "We can have our stuff shipped and call Nana Dottie from the road. I'm sure she'll understand."

Momma releases a sigh so long I wonder if she's been holding her breath since leaving HauteCoco. After a few seconds, she checks the rearview mirror, steers the car to the side of the road, and stops.

"We're not going back to Kansas," she says, looking at me.

"Oh. Okay. You just seemed upset, and then you said we were going home, so I thought that's what you meant."

"It wasn't." She shakes her head. "Or maybe it was. I don't know."

I wait for her to offer more, but she doesn't. "What happened, Momma?" I ask finally. "What did Clementine say? Was she mean?"

She smiles, but it's a sad smile. "It just wasn't the job for me."

I nod, even though it's obvious that there was more to it than that.

"Anyway," she says with forced cheerfulness, "we knew it wouldn't be easy—and we were right. But when have Ruby and Francie Lee ever run away from a challenge?"

"We've taken a few detours before, but we always come back to meet it."

"Exactly." She takes my hand and squeezes it. "And speaking of detours, what do you say we grab some ice cream before heading back?"

"I'd say there's nothing a little mint chocolate chip can't fix."

Momma gives my hand another squeeze before releasing it. She puts the car in drive, checks the mirrors, and steps on the gas.

The car jolts forward, then stops.

The traffic must be pretty bad for Momma to hit the brake like that. I turn around and look out the back window to help find a good opening . . . but the road's nearly empty. We're also in a residential area, so the few cars on the road are moving very slowly.

Momma tries the gas again. We jerk forward a foot, then stop.

"Are we out of gas?" I ask.

"We have half a tank." She keeps one foot on the brake and steps on the gas with her other foot three times, letting it linger on the last. The engine responds, but softens from a roar to a rumble the longer she holds down the pedal.

"It might be the battery," she says.

"Do we have a charger?"

"We have jumper cables, but those don't help without another battery to attach them to."

She tries driving three more times. On the third attempt, the engine seems to yawn, like it's preparing for a long nap, and then falls silent.

I look at Momma. Her fingers are white around the steering wheel again. She's staring straight ahead, not blinking. I would never say so, but I can't help but think how much easier this situation would be if we had a cell phone. We could call a garage or Nana Dottie, and we'd be back on the road in no time.

"Should we get out and try to find a gas station?" I ask after a long, quiet moment. "Or knock on people's doors and see if someone will let us use their phone?"

"This isn't Curly Creek, Ruby." Momma's voice is tense. "People here just aren't as nice as they were back home."

I frown. Momma always thinks the best of everyone, no matter where they're from . . . which means Clementine must've given her reason to think otherwise.

"Can I help?"

And then, as if he sensed Momma could use a reminder that kindness does exist outside Curly Creek, Oscar smiles at her through the driver's side window.

13.

I've never felt more like Dorothy than when we first enter Oscar's flower shop.

"This is your *office*?" I ask, since that's where he said we were going when we climbed into his delivery van ten minutes ago.

"It has a computer and a phone," he says, like he doesn't know why I wouldn't believe him. Except he's smiling—so I know he knows why I wouldn't.

If somewhere over the rainbow really did exist, Oscar's flower shop would be it. Something magical happens the second your feet leave the ordinary gray sidewalk and step through the doorway. Colors that seemed bright and vibrant outside, like the green of the grass and blue of the sky, fade to black and white as soon as you're inside. Because the flower shop is *filled* with color. Red, pink, purple, orange, yellow, blue, green, turquoise, fuchsia, peach, and about a million other shades I've never even seen before pop from floor to ceiling. There are roses, daisies, lilies, sunflowers, tulips, lilacs, orchids, and hydrangeas—and those are only the flowers I recognize. There also are flowerless plants with leaves so green they don't even need blossoms, as well as lemon trees and orange trees. Scattered among the flowers and trees are stone fountains with trickling water and separate, small bird baths with real live birds dancing along the edges.

The other side of the rainbow, with its gray sidewalk and dirty roads, is only inches away . . . but you'd never know it from here.

"Momma, have you ever seen anything like it?" My voice is barely a whisper.

"No, Ruby. I definitely haven't." She sounds awed too but then seems to remember why we're here and turns to Oscar. "If you could just point me toward your phone . . . ?"

"You know, I have some tools in the back," Oscar says. "I'd be happy to take a closer look at the car so you don't have to bring someone out."

"Thank you," Momma says. "But you already tried jump-starting the battery and were kind enough to give us a ride. I really don't want to impose."

"You're not imposing. In fact, you'd be doing me a favor. The van's always acting up, and after too many trips to the shop I'm trying to teach myself what mechanics don't want me to know. It'd be good practice."

This sounds like a great idea to me, but Momma's not convinced. She's already weaving her way through the indoor garden, apparently in search of the phone.

"She's very independent," I explain when Oscar looks at me.

"Be sure to check out the pond," he says as he starts

after her. "It's a work-in-progress, but I think you'll like it."

They disappear into a miniature forest of trees with big yellow flowers before I can ask what he means. Deciding to take advantage of the chance to explore, I walk slowly through the store, stopping every few inches to sniff and take pictures. I take so many I finish the roll of film and have to load another—which I'm very glad I have, since Oscar was right about the pond.

It's in a large room off the main showroom, and if it weren't for the shaded glass walls and ceiling, I'd think it was outside. It's about ten feet long by ten feet wide and surrounded by tall grass and pink, purple, and yellow flowers.

Wildflowers. They look just like the ones that line the banks of Curly Creek each spring.

I take a dozen pictures as I walk across a narrow footbridge. I stop in the middle to take more pictures of the brightly colored fish swimming below. A small mountain of white rocks sits at the other end of the bridge, next to a shovel and two bags of dirt. I assume these are for the next phase of Oscar's work-in-progress.

The pond is so pretty, so peaceful, I'm tempted to sit on the bridge and dangle my feet over the side. But as calm as I feel right now, I doubt Momma feels the same way after her stressful day. So I quickly snap a few more pictures before hurrying across the bridge and into the showroom.

"I don't understand."

I slow down when I spot Momma through a wide bouquet of orange tulips. She's still on the phone . . . and she doesn't sound happy.

"You have to *tow* the car? You can't try fixing it where it is?"

A tree rustles a few feet away. I peek through leaves to see Oscar trimming branches. I can tell he's trying not to listen to Momma's conversation, but his frown and furrowed brow give away his concern.

"Okay," Momma says. "If that's how you do it, then that's what we'll do. How much will the tow cost?"

Oscar catches my eye. I shrug. I don't know why she won't accept his help.

"Two hundred dollars?" Momma leans against the counter. She shakes her head slowly as she listens to the person on the other end of the phone. "Will you take a check?"

There's more rustling. I look over to see Oscar standing up after bending down to pick up the tree trimmers he just dropped.

"I don't have a credit card." Momma pauses. "What's a bank card? Never mind—I don't have that either. Will cash work? Or is Florida beyond that, too?"

Uh oh. Judging by her tone, Momma's just jumped from frustrated to mad.

"Oscar?" she calls out suddenly.

I cover my mouth to keep from giggling when he drops the trimmers again.

"I'm very sorry to bother you, but do you happen to know where you found us?"

There's a fresh wave of rustling as he brushes through the branches to get to her. As she gives him the phone and he gives the shop directions, I lift my camera and quickly take a few shots. Not only am I sure Momma will want to laugh about this moment later, when we're finally settled and all this is a distant memory, the image of her standing next to Oscar just makes for a good picture. She's tall, but he's two inches taller. Her skin, while tan for her, is creamy white compared to his. Her thin arms look delicate next to his, which aren't huge but still are muscular and strong. She's wearing her black skirt and camisole. In the stress of the moment she forgot her heels in our car, so her feet are bare. He's wearing jeans, a red polo shirt, and leather sandals. They look completely different, totally mismatched, like two random socks grabbed from a messy drawer . . . except for their faces. She looks worried but grateful. He looks the same.

"An *hour*?" Momma says when Oscar hangs up. "Why on earth will it take so long?"

"They're backed up, short-staffed, and who knows what else. Are you sure you don't want me to take a look? If I fix it, we can cancel the tow before they've even left."

"No, that's okay." Momma's face softens. "But thank

you. It's so nice of you to help out a couple of total strangers."

"You're not total strangers. You're the daughter and granddaughter of my toughest Scrabble competitor. If I take good care of you, maybe Dictionary Dottie will go easy on me the next time we play."

I smile when Momma laughs. "I doubt that," she says.

"Are you hungry?" Oscar turns and ducks, looking for me through the leaves. "I can order some food."

"Actually, we should probably get going. If you don't mind my borrowing your phone again, I'll call Dictionary Dottie and ask her to pick us up. I'm sure Ruby has homework, and we don't want to take up any more of your time."

"It's Saturday," I say, popping out from behind the tulips. "Homework is for Sundays."

Momma looks surprised. Oscar looks hopeful.

"Plus, after doing seven laps around HauteCoco, I'm starving." I look at Momma and shrug. We both know she can't stand between food and me.

"HauteCoco, huh?" Oscar says, reaching for the phone book. "Doing some shopping?"

"Yes," I say.

"No," Momma says at the same time. I look at her again, and now *she* shrugs. "I was trying to find a job. But if you say one word to my mother I'll make sure the only easy thing about your next Scrabble game is the way she beats you."

Oscar laughs. Momma smiles. Not long ago it seemed like nothing would make her feel better about the afternoon—not even ice cream, though I thought it was worth a try. But now she's joking about it. And all it took was Oscar.

"So what'll it be?" he asks. "Chinese? Mexican? Italian? All of the above?"

"I could really go for an egg roll," I say, patting my stomach, "but I could *also* really go for a slice of pepperoni."

"And I'm kind of feeling like a fajita," Momma says apologetically.

This kind of culinary indecision isn't unusual for us;

most people who didn't know that would probably find it strange — if not annoying. But Oscar grins. "An international smorgasbord it is. Write down what you want, and I'll order."

Twenty minutes later, we're having a picnic by Oscar's pond — which, we learn, he built himself. We also learn that he prefers smaller, quieter bodies of water to the ocean, which just about makes Momma and me choke on our garlic knots. Up until when he said this, we thought we were the only ones in Florida who felt that way.

And that's not the only surprise. Oscar loves old movies, especially anything with Audrey or Katharine Hepburn, who just happen to be two of my favorite actresses of all time. He watches *The Wizard of Oz* with his nieces every Thanksgiving. He grew up with his mom and four sisters, so he understands the special bond between a mother and daughter. (Thankfully, this part of the conversation manages to stay away from the special bond between Momma and Nana Dottie.) He started working while he was in high school. He learned business from his uncle Paulo, who owned a tobacco store, and his love of flowers from weekend visits to the neighborhood park with his grandparents. He's never been married and doesn't have kids—unless you count Bessie, his chocolate lab, which we do.

He also loves music. Old music. Like the kind Momma and I listen to, not the loud, thumping kind everyone at Sweet Citrus listens to. We learn *this* when "Sweet Caroline" by Neil Diamond comes on the radio and Oscar immediately jumps up and holds out both hands.

"Oh. No. I can't." Momma shakes her head when she realizes what he's doing.

"Maybe later," I groan lightly. "When the food digests."

Our laziness doesn't stop him. He sings and dances around the pond, over the bridge, and by the pile of rocks and dirt. He sings and dances about as well as Momma and I do—which isn't well at all—and the great thing is, he doesn't seem to care. What he definitely does care about is having fun. A minute into the song he looks like he's having so much of it that I get up and join him. Another thirty seconds after that, Momma follows. We shuffle, wiggle, and laugh. Every now and then Momma spins me, Oscar spins her, and I spin him. Whenever my hands are free I take a few pictures that I'm sure will be fuzzy, since I don't stand still long enough to make sure they're not.

"So," Oscar says when we collapse on the grass, exhausted, three songs later. "Tell me about Curly Creek. What's it like? How big is it? What was your favorite thing to do there? What do you miss most about it?"

Momma and I look at each other. We could spend hours talking about Curly Creek . . . and I have a feeling that eventually, we will with Oscar. But this doesn't feel like the right time.

"Usually we miss everything," Momma says, taking my hand. "But right now . . . ?"

I smile. I know she wants me to answer, just to make sure I feel the same way. And as much as I've missed

Gabby, our house, and our old life, and as much as I'll probably miss Curly Creek later tonight and tomorrow and the day after that, I *do* feel the same way.

"Right now?" I squeeze Momma's hand. "Not much."

14.

As predicted, it doesn't take long to start missing Curly Creek again. Thirty-six hours after our impromptu pond dance with Oscar, I'm sitting in the backseat of Nana Dottie's Jaguar, wishing I were two thousand miles away.

"Are you sure there's nowhere else we can try?" I ask.

"Sweetie, it's eight in the morning," Momma says. "The stores don't open for another two hours."

"One of my friends from the club has a friend whose

cousin's husband's sister has a dance shop in Key Biscayne. I could give her a ring and see if she'll open early for us."

"Would you?" I sit up and stick my head between the two front seats. "I'd really appreciate it, Nana Dottie."

"It would be my pleasure, Ruby." Nana Dottie takes her cell phone from the cup holder and starts dialing.

"Mom," Momma says, her voice firm. "It's *eight* in the *morning*. That's really early, even for your set."

Nana Dottie lowers the phone. "And what set would that be, Francine? The senior set? The cane-and-walker set? The gee-I-wish-I-still-had-my-teeth set?"

"I meant your friends, Mom," Momma says, trying not to roll her eyes. "Eight in the morning is really early, even for your friends who play tennis before they eat breakfast."

"It's okay, Nana Dottie. Even if your friend's friend's husband's . . ." I give up. "Even if your contact is awake, we don't really have time to drive to Key Biscayne and back. It's bad enough I look like this. I can't look like this *and* be late."

"I think you look adorable," Momma says, turning in her seat to smile at me. "Very professional."

"You know, there's a lovely studio in Coral Gables." Nana Dottie starts dialing again. "They must have early rehearsals, and I bet they sell—"

"Hang up the phone, Mom. Ruby doesn't want to be late, and neither do I. If we leave in the next sixty seconds, we'll make it to the garage just in time for me to pick up the car and get to my appointment."

"Right. Your appointment." Nana Dottie turns off the phone and replaces it in the cupholder. "What's that for again?"

I temporarily forget my own troubles. I'm curious to know where Momma's going too. She hasn't said much about it, so I'm hoping it's somewhere with Oscar.

"You look great," Momma says to me, ignoring Nana Dottie. "I promise."

I don't believe her but don't have much of a choice. The second bell has already rung, and the front lawn is nearly empty. As I lift my backpack and slide out of the car, I remind myself that at least I won't be the only one who looks like she rode to school in a tiny clown car.

"Break a leg!" Momma calls after me.

I'm about to cross the street when Nana Dottie rolls down her window.

"Ruby, take this." She unties the long yellow scarf that's around her neck and reaches it through the window. "Just in case."

"Thanks." Personally, I think adding to my outfit will only make it worse, but I take the scarf anyway. Once I do, Nana Dottie smiles, Momma blows me a kiss, and they start to drive away. I wait until the Jaguar rounds the corner down the street before stuffing the scarf in my backpack.

"Well, hi there, Tiny Dancer!" Mr. Fox says when I reach the metal detectors.

Despite my bad mood, I can't help but smile. "Morning, Mr. Fox. You like Elton John?"

"I like lots of singers, Dorothy. Now tell me, what's the occasion?"

I take out my lunch box and camera and pass them

through the doorway. "Citrus Star. Everyone in my group is wearing their rehearsal outfits all day. It's supposed to help us 'mentally prepare for infinite fame.' Or something."

"Looking the part can only help you feel the part," he says, snatching my stuff as quickly as we'd practiced last week. "Why do you think I put on this silly blue security uniform every day? It's hot as heck, but if I showed up in shorts and a T-shirt, I might relax on the job, and then who knows what you kids would do."

"Go to class?" I guess.

"You're all right, Dorothy." He chuckles. "How many members does your group have?"

"Five. Including me." I pass through the doorway.

"So I should've seen four others come through here this morning?"

"If they were on time, yes." I take my camera and lunch box.

"Huh."

I glance up from my backpack. Mr. Fox seems puzzled. "They probably looked a little different," I explain. "Not quite as . . . bright."

"Actually—"

The bell cuts him off.

"Have to run," I say, hurrying down the hallway. "Have a great day!"

As I jog toward homeroom, I can't decide if it's good or bad that I'm late. The halls are nearly empty, which significantly limits the number of curious looks I get, but that just means everyone's already in classrooms and that the looks will hit me all at once. At least Ava and the rest of Constellation have already made their public appearances. Mine will still be different, but it shouldn't come as a total shock.

Except that it does. I stand in the homeroom doorway, unable to move under the pressure of twenty pairs of eyes.

"Laundry day?" a high-pitched voice asks from the back of the room. Stephanie's question is followed by a series of snorts and giggles.

I force my neck to turn. My head's swirling so I can't tell one thought from the next, but somewhere in there I already know what's happened. Unfortunately, that doesn't keep the truth from stinging once I look it in the face.

"Missed you at rehearsal this morning," Ava Grand says. *She* looks mad at *me*—even though I'm the one in a clown costume, and she's wearing another pretty sundress. Stephanie and Hilary giggle on either side of her. They're also wearing regular clothes. I want to look for Megan, but moving once is apparently all my neck is willing to do.

"Ruby?" Mr. Soto says gently. "The Pledge is about to start. Why don't you take a seat?"

Little does Mr. Soto know that if only I could feel my feet, sitting at my desk in this room would be the last thing I'd do. I'd be running after Nana Dottie's Jaguar so fast, I'd catch up with it before it even reached the highway.

"Oh, look. Luis Lobo's Hummer is pulling into the parking lot."

The room explodes. Some kids gasp. Others squeal. Chair legs screech against the floor. Books topple off desks. I think Luis Lobo must be some sort of Floridian

Santa Claus and his Hummer the warm-weather equivalent of a sleigh filled with millions of presents. Because everyone pushes and nudges their way to the wall of windows.

Everyone, that is, but Sam.

He's still sitting at his desk, looking at me instead of out the windows. For a second I'm mortified that with the entire class on the other side of the room, he has a clear view of my circus ensemble. But then I realize he's not looking at my clothes. His eyes don't leave mine. He gives me a half smile and shakes his head slightly, and I know that whoever Luis Lobo is, he's not pulling into the school parking lot. Sam just said that so I could walk to my desk and sit down without everyone watching, whispering, and giggling.

I dash to my desk, surprisingly grateful for the footwear portion of my outfit. The jazz shoes might be orange with black tiger stripes, but at least they're quiet. I'm already seated and pulling out a notebook when the class starts trickling away from the windows.

"Luis Lobo isn't out there," one kid says.

"Maybe he was, but then he left before we could see him," another says.

"You know how secretive he is," a third adds. "He'll probably hide in the auditorium and watch rehearsals this afternoon."

This guess prompts more gasps and squeals. I'm pretty sure I hear Ava Grand whispering frantically to the rest of Constellation, but I don't care. Even when I think I'm in the loop I'm not, so there's no point trying to listen.

Instead, I continue my letter to Gabby, which is currently fourteen pages long. At this rate, I'll need to mail it in a box instead of an envelope.

My pencil freezes when a crumpled paper ball lands in the middle of my notebook. My body has barely recovered from its initial paralysis, and now it's tense again. I wait for more, for a paper snowball attack brought on by—what? Silly clothes? Looking different? Being the new girl? If these are my biggest crimes, I hope I never really mess up here.

I don't think I'd make it out of the paper avalanche alive.

Five seconds go by. Ten. Twenty. After thirty seconds pass without another hit, I think I might be okay. Maybe that one wasn't even meant for me. I relax enough to brush the paper ball from my notebook.

Hey Ruby—

My eyes lock on the handwriting. Apparently, this paper ball *was* meant for me.

I look up and scan the room without moving my head. Everyone's discussing the supposed sighting of Luis Lobo and what it might mean. No one's watching me or waiting to see if I'll open the note.

So I do. At this point, what's the worst that can happen?

Hey Ruby—
What was that about?? Are you okay?
—S

S. Given her earlier laundry day comment, I'm guessing Stephanie's not too concerned about my well-being. Which means Sam is.

Gabby and I used to pass notes in class all the time, so this one shouldn't seem like such a big deal — especially after my morning trauma — but it does. And not just because it's from a cute boy who has the best name ever and who knows of Vivian Vance. That doesn't hurt . . . but it's a big deal mostly because it's the first note I've gotten since starting at Sweet Citrus.

Hey Sam. I guess Constellation decided to have some fun with their dullest "star." Thanks for distracting the class. I owe you one! —R
PS Who's Luis Lobo?

I quietly crumple the note back into a ball and wait for Mr. Soto to turn to the blackboard before tossing it toward Sam. It grazes his arm and lands on his desk. A minute later, it lands on mine.

L.L. is some hot-shot talent agent. He comes to Citrus Star every year looking for the next big thing. Much to Ava's dismay, he hasn't found it yet. By the way, I hate the spotlight too. (Though for what it's worth, you wear neon well.)

—S

I smile. If anyone else here said I wore neon well, I'd think they were making fun of me. Somehow, I know Sam's not like anyone else.

I want to continue our written conversation, but the bell rings before I can toss the ball back for another turn. I gather my stuff quickly, hoping Sam and I can walk to first period together, but by the time my backpack's zipped, he's already gone.

And unfortunately, no one outside of our homeroom was alerted to Luis Lobo's fake presence. Which means everyone is immediately alerted to my very real, very noticeable presence as I head down the hallway.

"Tell me you didn't check your e-mail this morning."

I look up from my tiger-striped jazz shoes to see

Megan walking next to me. "I know it's kind of the thing to do here, but I can't lie."

She groans, takes my elbow, and steers me toward a restroom. I'm relieved when it's another single-person-only restroom.

"She said she e-mailed you about our rehearsal this morning." Megan locks the door and turns toward me.

"Who said?" I can guess, but I want to hear Megan say it. As nice as I thought she was a few days ago, right now, in her pretty sundress and metallic sandals, she's no different from her friends.

"Ava." She goes to the sink and drops her silver tote bag on the counter. "She sent the e-mail last night about rehearsal after school today, and I saw you were copied on it. But then she texted us all this morning to say plans had changed and that we were rehearsing *before* school."

"Texted?" I ask, watching her rummage through her bag.

"Sent notes. To our cell phones."

"I don't have a cell phone."

She looks up, surprised. After a second, she

returns to her bag. "Well, at the very least, I knew that if you had a cell phone she didn't have your number. So I texted her back and asked if she'd e-mailed you about the change, and she swore she did. She also said she could tell that you'd opened and read the note."

"You can do that?"

"I can't. But Ava seems to know how to do lots of things other people don't." She pulls a pair of flip-flops from her bag.

"I only got two e-mails," I say. "Both were sent yesterday. One was about rehearsing this afternoon. The other said she'd talked to Miss Anita and that I was definitely in the group, and that we were all wearing our rehearsal outfits to school. It also included a very specific list of what I needed for my rehearsal outfit and where I should get everything."

She frowns at me in the mirror above the sink. "And where was that?"

"Coco Costumes—which actually had a very limited selection. I thought black leotards, pink leg warmers, white tights, and black jazz shoes would be easy to find, but the store didn't have any of them."

She digs in her purse again and yanks out a tank top.

"Anyway, I got that e-mail late yesterday afternoon, so by the time we got to Coco Costume and learned they didn't have what I needed, everywhere else was closed. And I thought it was better to show up in some sort of dance outfit than none at all, so . . ."

I turn and face the full-length mirror. I don't know how Momma and Nana Dottie let me leave the house like this. I was too embarrassed to check my appearance this morning, but the outfit looks even more ridiculous than I imagined. But then, how could I look anything *but* ridiculous in a neon-yellow leotard with silver sequins, green leg warmers with pink fringe, purple tights, and tiger-striped jazz shoes?

"This was all they had," I explained reluctantly.

"Of course it was. Coco Costumes is for Halloween, not for Citrus Star—or for any other kind of legitimate performance. I wouldn't be surprised if Ava even went there before e-mailing you just to make sure they didn't have what she told you to get."

I shake my head. "But why? Why would she do that? What have I done to her to make her dislike me so much?"

"Nothing. Except move here and take attention away from her."

"That's impossible," I say automatically. "I haven't done anything to take attention from her. I couldn't even if I tried."

"You're new." Megan joins me in front of the mirror and places the flip-flops on the floor next to my feet. "That's enough right there. But you're also nice and funny and sincere—three things Ava Grand will probably never be."

I eye the tank top she holds toward me. "What's that for?"

"I can't get through a meal without half of it ending up on my clothes, so I always bring backups. If I hadn't spilled chocolate milk on my first dress of the day before homeroom, I'd give you the one I'm wearing now."

"And you were just going to wear a tank top if you spilled something on this dress at lunch?"

She smiles. "If I spill anything else, I may have to go home sick. This is from last week. My shirt and shoes were spared when a plate of spaghetti fell on my lap at lunch on Friday, and I forgot to take those backups out of my bag."

I look at her. "You really want to loan me your clothes?"

"I really do. It's the least I can do for underestimating Ava." She reaches into her purse again and removes a square plastic box. She opens it, pulls something out, and hands it to me. "Take this too. It always helps me feel better."

I take it, too stunned to speak.

Because it's a cassette tape. The square plastic box was a Walkman . . . just like mine.

"It's the *Mamma Mia!* soundtrack," she says. "I know this great company that converts iTunes files to tapes. Most people think it's crazy, but I think music sounds better this way, don't you?"

"Definitely," I say, even though I'm not sure what an iTune is.

She smiles and grabs her purse. "Anyway, I have to

run—I have kindergarten math today, which is on the other side of the building. See you at lunch?"

She's through the door before I can respond. I'm still looking at the cassette tape when the door flings open again.

"By the way," Megan says, popping her head into the room, "there's one other thing you are that Ava Grand will probably never be."

Short? Average? Technologically challenged?

"Brave." She grins and then disappears.

I lock the door and reach for my backpack. As I dig around for my camera, I'm excited to find Nana Dottie's yellow scarf. I'd forgotten about it, but it's long enough to wrap around my waist and wear as a skirt, and it will look great with Megan's white tank top and flip-flops.

I can't wait to change, but there's something I need to do first.

I don't know if I'm brave. I certainly don't *feel* very brave—especially not in Coconut Grove. But just in case Megan sees something in me that I don't, I want to take a picture to examine for clues later.

15. "So then Andy do-si-dos Brian, and Brian do-si-dos Clint, and Clint do-si-dos Justin, and around and around it goes until they all get so dizzy they slip away from one another, stumble across the barn floor, and crash into bales of hay."

Giggling, I step onto the diving board.

"And it's not confirmed, but we think someone did something to the punch, because after a few cups, Mr. Lou's words started running together. Which was pretty dangerous, since he was calling the square dancing and people started running into each other when they couldn't make out his instructions."

"Did anyone get hurt?" I ask, bouncing gently.

"Physically, not really," Gabby says. "Emotionally,

definitely. I'm still recovering from the image of macho-man Clint wearing cowboy boots and skipping to country music."

"It sounds like it was everything we always thought it'd be."

"Well, not *quite* everything, since our very first boy-girl dance of junior high was missing one key guest." Gabby pauses. "Are you, like, exercising or something?"

I sit up on the pile of pillows on the grass, where I landed with a thud after jumping off the diving board. "You heard that?"

"I think Momma Kibben heard it, and she's down at the high school for karaoke night. It sounds like you're running hurdles or doing the long jump. Have those outdoorsy sports nuts turned you into an athlete already?"

I smile. Gabby asks this like athletes are also criminals. "Don't worry, I'm as muscle-free as I was the last time you saw me. I'm just practicing for Citrus Star."

"Citrus Star? What's that?"

"The talent show? Featuring all my fame-obsessed classmates?" I hop on the diving board again. "I must've told you about it."

"I don't think so. We haven't really talked lately."

I stop bouncing. Can that be right? Have we really not talked since I started rehearsing? "I don't want us to be so busy that we can't find time to call and then don't know what's going on in each other's lives."

"Me neither. What about that letter? Weren't you trying to break the world record for longest note ever written?"

"Yes." I start bouncing again. "I think I broke it three weeks ago. And I'll mail the letter tomorrow. It might take you a few days to finish it, but when you do, you'll know absolutely everything about life in Coconut Grove."

"And what about pictures? Will you send some of those, too? So I can have visuals while I read?"

I wince. "Those might take a little longer. I haven't gotten to the drugstore to develop them yet."

"You know . . . if we e-mailed, we could update each

other every day. And then you could put your pictures on a CD and I could look at them three seconds after you send them."

"True." I bounce once more, bend my knees, and leap from the diving board. I watch my reflection in the sliding glass door as I sail through the air and drop to the ground. "But I still hate e-mail—probably more now than ever. Let's just promise to talk on the phone at least every other day."

"Good idea. Cross my heart."

"Me too."

After we hang up, I continue jumping off the diving board. There's one thirty-second stretch in Constellation's routine that's nothing but jumping. We did a run-through this afternoon, and it turns out that just as I'm the group's worst singer and dancer, I'm also its worst jumper. When Ava saw how stiff my legs were, she threw up her hands and stormed out of the auditorium for an extended break. But Megan assured me that stiff legs can limber up, and she gave me a few pointers—including this diving board technique. I think it's working, too. After a dozen jumps, my reflection's head disappears above the glass.

"Ruby, would you like a snack?"

"No thanks, Nana Dottie!" I bounce three times and jump again. "No time for food."

Nana Dottie called to me through the kitchen window. A few seconds later, she opens the sliding glass door and strides across the patio. When she reaches me, she puts both hands on my shoulders to stop my bouncing and then holds one palm to my forehead.

"You don't have a fever," she says, relieved.

"I feel fine," I say, surprised.

She raises her eyebrows. "I know we haven't been living together for very long, but in that time, I've never once heard you refuse food."

She has a point. And now that I'm standing still, I realize I am a little hungry. "Do you have anything light? Something that will keep my energy up?"

Her whole face breaks into a smile, like I've just offered to give up chips for tofu forever. "Come with me."

I follow her inside. I swing by the desk in the living

room to pick up my laptop and continue on into the kitchen.

"Hi, Oscar." I smile, then cover my mouth when I see what he's doing. "Sorry," I whisper through my fingers.

"Don't be." He looks up from the Scrabble board, leans back in his chair, and grins. "I'm always happy to see my favorite Kansas sunflower."

This is one of the things I love about Oscar. He can do things like call me a Kansas sunflower, which might sound silly if anyone else said it, and make it seem like the easiest, most natural thing in the world.

"Plus, your grandmother is currently destroying me. My brain could use a break." He nods to my laptop. "Doing some homework?"

"Sort of." I put the computer on the kitchen table and open it. "I'm rehearsing for Citrus Star."

"Ah, yes. The beloved tween variety show. I hear MTV is doing a live broadcast of it this year."

I fall into a chair. "Please tell me you're kidding."

He winks. "I am."

"Ruby's a member of Constellation, the popular

singing and dancing group that's going for a third first-place victory," Nana Dottie says proudly as she bustles about the kitchen.

"Nice." Oscar sounds impressed.

"Yeah. No pressure or anything." I turn on the computer and load the Internet. "Want to see what crazy things I have to convince my body to do in eighteen days?"

"Are there diagrams?" Oscar asks, scooting over his chair.

"Even better—or worse, depending on how you look at it."

"Is that video?" Nana Dottie comes around the counter for a closer look. "Of Ava Grand?"

"The one and only." I shake my head as Ava glides across the screen. "She hired a choreographer to help with the routine, a videographer to record her performing the routine, and some kind of website genius to put it online."

"What if someone else from school finds it?" Oscar asks. "And tries to copy your moves?"

"It would be like trying to find a diamond in a dust

storm. The video link is hidden in all sorts of fake websites, and you need four different passwords to load it."

Nana Dottie pats my shoulder before returning to snack preparations. I know she's proud of the tech-savvy words I'm throwing out, like "link," "websites," and "passwords." It doesn't seem like a big deal now, but I guess compared to a few weeks ago, when I didn't even know how to find the Internet on my computer, it kind of is.

"Ouch," Oscar says as Ava does a hands-free cartwheel and lands in a split.

"You're telling me," I say.

"You're going to be great," Nana Dottie says. "It's a challenge, but you're in extremely talented company. And there's no better teacher than Ava Grand."

I think that last point's debatable but don't say so. "The hardest part is actually the music. My body's never done half this stuff, but it's learning—slowly. The bigger problem is putting the moves to music. What we're dancing to is just so different from what I'm used to."

"I can see that," Oscar says, his head bobbing with the beat. "Is this Beyoncé? With Jay-Z? The radio remix?"

I look at him. "How did you know that?"

"My nieces are nuts for this stuff. It's pretty good, once you get used to it. And you *do* get used to it, believe it or not."

"He's right, Ruby." Nana Dottie places a tray of strawberries, blueberries, whole-wheat pita wedges, and guacamole on the table. "You just need another lesson."

"You know pop music, Nana Dottie?"

She bites into a strawberry. "You'd be surprised. We'll start with an iPod. And lots of CDs. You can load the CDs into iTunes, sync iTunes to your iPod, and listen to music whenever you want, wherever you are."

"I'm sorry."

I jump in my chair. We all turn to see Momma standing in the kitchen doorway.

"An iPod? iTunes? What kind of technological takeover are you planning without my consent this time, Mom?"

"Momma?" I stand up. "Are you okay? You look . . . hot. And sick."

"After walking two miles in the blazing hot sun, yes,

I'm a bit warm. And after the day I've had, I do feel rather nauseous." She tears a paper towel from the roll on the counter and blots her damp face.

"Of course you're hot," Nana Dottie says. "It's ninety degrees out, and you're wearing that heavy black suit."

Momma looks at Nana Dottie. Nana Dottie looks at Momma. Each seems to be daring the other to speak, but neither wants to be the first to give.

"How about some water?" Oscar finally asks, reaching for the beverage cart next to the table.

The movement breaks their silent stare. Nana Dottie sits down and turns her attention to the Scrabble board. Momma takes off her jacket and fans her face with a spatula. Oscar hands me the glass of water to take across the kitchen, and I wait until Momma finishes it before speaking again.

"Why did you walk two miles?" It seems like an obvious question to me, and I'm not sure why it's taken this long for someone to ask it.

Momma swallows the last of the water and takes a deep breath. "The car died."

"*Again?* But you just picked it up this morning. I thought it was fixed."

"So did I. And it got me everywhere I needed to go today, but on the way home, it just stopped in the middle of the street. In the middle of rush-hour traffic. Which won me lots of points with our professional new neighbors, since going around me—and then around me *and* the tow truck when it came—made everything move that much slower."

"That's terrible." Oscar gets up from the table and stands across the counter from Momma. He's immediately concerned, which is more than can be said for Nana Dottie, who continues to plan her next Scrabble strategy. "Where's the car now? Can I take a look?"

"It's right outside. You can look if you want, but the mechanic said it's as dead as a doornail. The only way to bring it back to life is with a new engine. And even then there are no guarantees, since the car's so old and its parts are so rare."

"They brought the car all the way back here but

made you *walk*?" I ask in disbelief. That would never happen in Curly Creek.

"They offered me a ride, but I wanted to walk." Momma gives me a small smile. "I thought it would help clear my head."

"It sounds like you need all the help you can get in that department," Nana Dottie says without looking up from her tiles. "What did you think would happen to that rusty pile of scrap metal? It's a miracle it got you here from Kansas. It's done its job; now let it rest in peace."

Momma squeezes the water glass so tightly I brace for sharp flying shards.

"I'll be back." Oscar pats Momma's other hand, which is turning white against the counter.

"How was school today, sweetie?" she asks when he leaves the kitchen. Her voice is warm but tired. "And rehearsal?"

"School was fine," I say, still worried but willing to distract her for now. "And rehearsal was—"

"She needs an iPod."

I spin around. Nana Dottie's holding a strawberry

in one hand and rearranging tiles with the other.

"There are certain things Ruby needs to know in order to be successful here and in life. Music is one of them."

"Ruby knows music," Momma says. "We listen to records and tapes all the time."

"*Your* records," Nana Dottie says pointedly. "*Your* tapes. The poor girl's stuck in a disco time warp while her peers fly toward the future."

I glance at Momma. She's looking at Nana Dottie, eyes wide, mouth open.

"And while we're at it, you need a new car." Nana Dottie's voice is light, matter-of-fact.

"*No*, I don't," Momma says.

"Oh? Then how do you suppose you'll make it to all these mysterious appointments of yours? Walking? Skipping? Closing your eyes and magically teleporting yourself there?"

"I'll get a new engine. That'll just have to do for now."

"A new engine costs three thousand dollars. Do you have three thousand dollars, Francine? To spend on something that will only end up costing you even more money?"

"Then I'll rent a car. Or take the bus. I'll figure it out." Despite a second glass of water, Momma's sweating more now than she was when she first came inside.

"Renting a car will set you back a thousand dollars a month. The public transportation system is completely unreliable. And while I give you credit for figuring out many things on your own, this is different. Your *life* is different. Changes need to be made — before it's too late."

Questions zip through my head like silver beads in a pinball machine. What kind of changes? Before it's too late for what? And why are Nana Dottie and Momma speaking to each other like enemies instead of like mother and daughter?

"I have an idea," I say before either can launch another attack. "There are two perfectly good cars in the garage right now. Maybe Momma can borrow the Jaguar for a little while? Just until she decides what to do about our car? And maybe Nana Dottie can drive the yellow convertible, just until the situation's resolved?"

Personally, I think this is a perfect solution and one

of the best ideas I've ever had. I almost expect Momma to dash around the counter, Nana Dottie to jump out of her chair, and both of them to embrace me in a big grateful hug.

So I'm really surprised when Momma excuses herself and goes outside. And Nana Dottie stands up, says she's going for a drive, and disappears into the garage. And I'm suddenly in the kitchen, all by myself.

After a few minutes, when no one returns, I sit down and try watching the Citrus Star routine online. Thirty seconds in, I decide I'm too distracted to focus. I think about calling Gabby, but I don't really want Momma or Nana Dottie accidentally overhearing our conversation, so I find my notebook and continue my letter to her instead.

That doesn't work either. All I can think about is what just happened and what it might mean. And since what it might mean is Momma and Nana Dottie never getting along and us going back to Kansas and Nana Dottie living alone the rest of her life, I close my notebook. There must be a way to work it out. We just have to be honest and talk about it, as difficult as that may be.

I head for the front door. I start to open it but stop when I hear laughter coming from outside. Peering through the window next to the door, I see Momma and Oscar standing next to our car. The hood's propped up, but they seem to have forgotten what's inside. Oscar leans against the driver's side door, talking, smiling, and waving a wrench around. Momma leans against the back door on the same side, one hand on her chest and her head thrown back as she laughs.

I grin. This is promising. Besides with me, Momma seems more like herself with Oscar than with anyone else here. Maybe he'll keep her relaxed enough to handle Nana Dottie.

Instantly reassured, I skip back through the kitchen toward the garage. I haven't heard a car start or the garage door open, so I assume Nana Dottie's still searching for her keys in her purse or adjusting her mirrors, which she does every time she gets in the Jaguar. I'll just ask her to stay and see if we can get to the bottom of this before it gets any worse.

I open the kitchen door that leads to the garage—and

then immediately close it. Because I was wrong. Nana Dottie's not getting ready to drive away in the Jaguar. She's sitting in the passenger seat of Papa Harry's yellow convertible.

And she's crying.

16.

"One-two, one-two-three. Kick, bend, jump-squat-shake."

I follow Ava's instructions. I'm so focused on matching the moves to the music booming overhead I barely see my reflection in the floor-to-ceiling mirror lining one wall of her bedroom.

"Faster, Stephanie! Sharper, Hilary!"

I scan the mirror's length. Whatever mistakes Ava's seeing must be visible only to a trained, professional eye. According to *my* eye, we look pretty good. Our movements are crisp yet fluid. We're in perfect sync. And despite going into our third straight hour of rehearsal, we smile like we've never been happier.

"Sloppy feet, Megan!"

I try not to cringe as I wait for my turn. Any time I haven't been spending eating, sleeping, studying, or rehearsing with Constellation in the past ten days, I've been rehearsing on my own. I fall asleep replaying the routine in my head, dream of standing ovations, and wake up early to rehearse some more. I sing in the shower and practice the arm choreography in the car. Momma thinks I'm going overboard, but I think I can't do enough. If I'm laughed off the stage during Citrus Star, I don't want it to be because I didn't try.

"Ruby . . . not bad."

This, of course, almost makes me trip on my feet and fall to the plush pink carpet. Not bad? That's the highest praise I've heard Ava Grand give anyone but herself.

We do the routine three more times. Ava's just about to start the music from the beginning again when there's a knock on the door. A tall woman with light blond hair enters the room. She's wearing a floor-length, strapless black sundress, silver sandals, and more diamonds than the Curly Creek Jewel Box has probably sold in its entire existence. As she walks, her jewelry catches the sunlight, making her glitter from head to toe.

"Hi, Mom," Ava says.

I'm standing still now, but almost trip on my feet again and fall to the plush pink carpet. This woman is Ava's *mother*? She looks young enough to be a big sister.

"Everyone's gathered on the lawn," Mrs. Grand says. "Are we ready?"

"As ready as we can possibly be, considering." Ava walks to the mirrored wall and fixes her hair. "How's the space?"

"Done exactly as you requested. Your father oversaw the process."

"Good." Ava puckers up and applies a fresh coat of lip gloss. "Daddy wouldn't accept anything but the best."

"I'll let our guests know the performance is about to begin."

"What performance?" Megan asks when Mrs. Grand leaves the room.

Ava gives Megan a small, sad smile in the mirror, like Megan's a baby bird that just can't figure out how to work her wings. "Megan. Sweetie. You know we give a performance preview every year."

"Yes . . . but you usually tell us when it's happening." Megan sounds confused.

"You didn't know?" Ava turns to Stephanie and Hilary. "Did *you* know?"

"Yes," they both say innocently.

"I've known for weeks," Hilary adds, trying not to smile. "That's why rehearsal was here today."

"I thought rehearsal was here today because the auditorium is closed for cleaning," Megan says.

"I guess someone was so busy playing Little Miss Phantom of the Opera she misread the memo." Ava shrugs. "Nothing we can do about that now. What's that they say in your world? The show must go . . . ?"

"On," Megan mumbles, looking at her feet.

"That's it." Ava grins and snaps her fingers, triumphant. "The show must go on. And so must we."

I squat down and pretend to tie my shoelace as Ava,

Stephanie, and Hilary file out of the room. When their whispers grow softer as they head downstairs, I look at Megan. She's pacing back and forth, wringing her hands.

"What's a performance preview?" I ask.

"A run-through of our routine for Ava's parents, her parents' friends, and her dad's colleagues. Ava's publicist says it's essential for generating buzz and getting feedback before the main event."

I want to ask what a publicist is and why Ava has one, but before I can, Megan makes a sudden U-turn and darts toward her tote bag.

"I just don't understand," she says, frantically sifting through her stuff. "Why did she tell them and not us? We've been to every rehearsal. We practice like crazy and don't complain. And she always *used* to tell me about things like this, so why not now? What did I do?"

I watch her turn her bag upside down and dump its contents onto the floor. "You were nice to me," I say, certain this is the reason. "When she didn't want to be, and when she didn't want anyone else to be. And lately we've been hanging out during breaks, which she doesn't seem to like either."

"But why not? What's the big deal? She should hang out with you too—you're so much fun."

This makes me smile, even though Ava's just pulled another one over on me and decided to punish Megan, too. The expression falls to a frown, though, when Megan pulls out her Walkman, puts on headphones, and leans against the mirror with her eyes closed.

"Um . . . Megan?" I say hesitantly. "Shouldn't we go downstairs?

"In a minute." She gently bobs her head. "I just need a minute."

I don't think we have that kind of time, but it's obvious she's not going anywhere in the next few seconds, so I distract myself from fear by taking a closer look around Ava's room.

Not surprisingly, it's big. Probably bigger than our whole house in Curly Creek. It's divided into three sections, which are like rooms without walls between them. There's a sleeping area with a king-sized canopy bed done in pink velvet and ivory silk. There's a living room area with two pink velvet couches, furry white pillows, and a TV hanging on the wall that's as big as the drive-in movie screen back home. And there's the area we've been practicing in, which has the mirrored wall, a ballet bar, and a retractable wooden dance floor. Off of that section is a pink marble bathroom and a walk-in closet that doubles as a guest bedroom when Ava's friends sleep over. I've never seen anything like it, and after today's performance, I probably won't ever again.

"Oh no," I whisper when I reach a set of French doors. They open onto a balcony overlooking the back-yard, but I don't have to go outside to see the yard filled with people. There must be dozens of them—maybe more. The men wear light-colored suits and the women wear beautiful sundresses. Waiters weave among them with trays of champagne and hors d'oeuvres. Rows of white wooden chairs face a long stage lined with bou-quets of flowers.

The flowers make me think of Oscar, and I wonder if he supplied them. If so, maybe he's still here. There's a tiny chance I won't die of embarrassment if I see at least one friendly face in the crowd.

"Thank you, Andrew."

I turn toward Megan, grateful for the reason to look away. She's wrapping the cord of her headphones around her Walkman. "Andrew?" I ask. "Is he a friend of yours?"

"Only in my wildest dreams." She seems much calmer as she replaces all of her belongings in her tote bag. "Andrew's Andrew Lloyd Webber, musical magician and composer of some of the best plays ever made."

"*Cats. Evita. Phantom of the Opera.*" For a quick second I regret speaking, since she seems so stunned I worry we won't ever make it downstairs. "My mom loves show tunes. I grew up listening to them."

"So you understand. Whenever I'm stressed, his music helps. It makes me so happy, I've even started composing some of my own."

My chin drops. "You know how to write music?"

"A little. I'm teaching myself, so it's a really slow process." She stands up and fixes her bun. "And it drives

Ava crazy, so I only work on it when she's not around. Since we've been rehearsing around the clock, that hasn't happened in a while."

I think about this as we head downstairs. We pause in front of one set of sliding glass doors and watch guests start taking their seats. From this angle I can see Ava backstage, barking orders in between vocal exercises.

"Why do you do it?" I ask quietly. "Why do you hang out with her and let her walk all over you? Wouldn't you rather spend that time doing what makes you happy?"

Megan doesn't look at me as her lips turn up in a small smile. "You know how the Scarecrow is totally lost until Dorothy comes along? And then when she does, he suddenly has friends and a purpose?"

"Yes," I say, even though I'm thinking that if Megan's comparing herself to a brainless sack of straw, the comparison isn't exactly accurate.

"That's what it's like with Ava."

Now I'm confused. "Ava's your Dorothy?"

"No," she says with a sigh. "She's my Great and Powerful Oz."

I want to remind Megan that the Great and Powerful Oz ends up being a not-so-great and powerless fake, but she's already sliding open the door and stepping outside. As I follow her across the yard, I wonder what it is about Ava that everyone loves so much. Sure, she's pretty. She has nice clothes. She can sing and dance. But is standing in the shadow of her spotlight worth not being yourself?

This has me so puzzled I don't remember to be terrified until we're standing backstage, waiting for the music to start.

"How many people do you think are out there?" I whisper to Megan, peering through a skinny opening in the pink velvet curtain.

"Eighty-four," Ava says before Megan can guess. She's sitting in a director's chair a few feet away, having her makeup done. "Twenty more than last year."

"Lucky me," I mutter, which makes Megan giggle.

"Is something funny?" Ava slides from the chair and joins us by the curtain. "Do I need to remind you how important this is? And how much better your lives will be if all goes the way it should? You can laugh now . . . but you'll be thanking me later."

I don't know about later, but right now I'm at least thankful for one thing: my rehearsal outfit. Nana Dottie bought a black leotard, fuzzy pink leg warmers, white tights, and black jazz shoes the day I wore the circus clothes to school, and thankfully, the outfit hasn't changed since. Knowing I look like the rest of the group helps me feel less self-conscious—and it is my only consolation as we take our positions.

"Smile, girls," Ava hisses from center stage as the music starts.

Once again, we do as we're told. It's hard to tell my hammering heart from the song's thudding bass, and my legs are shaking so hard I'm pretty sure they're making the stage vibrate, but I manage to hold the smile. It's still there as the curtain rises, revealing eighty-four people and a hundred and sixty-eight curious eyes. It's still there when the music gets louder and we're about to launch into our first dance sequence.

It disappears when I see Miss Anita.

She's sitting in the very last row, in the shade of a wide white parasol held by her assistant. Her face is expressionless and I can't see her eyes behind her sunglasses, but somehow I know she's watching me. She wants to make sure I haven't messed up the wonderful opportunity she gave me.

I try to tell myself to smile, but the words aren't there. My brain is as empty as Nana Dottie's Scrabble sack at the end of a game. There are no words. No sentences. No memories.

Nothing.

The music crescendos and Ava belts out her first note. Out of the corner of my eye I see the other girls start to move. They tilt their heads back. They lift their arms up and pull them down over and over, like they've lassoed the sun and want to bring it to earth. I've done the same move a million times over the last few weeks . . . but my body suddenly has no recollection.

A quick burst of light makes me think Constellation's functioning members have succeeded in lowering the sun. It's so bright I close my eyes against it. When the light dulls before my eyelids, I try opening them . . . and the light explodes again. Shielding my face with one hand, I glance at the girls. No one else seems to notice the ball of fire plummeting toward the stage, but everyone except Ava has noticed I'm not dancing. They're spinning in small circles, and each time they face me, they flash me different looks. Megan's is concern. Stephanie's and Hilary's are anger and shock, respectively.

I have to get off the stage. If I can just make it to the steps, they can finish the routine without my paralysis distracting the audience. Ava will hate me either way, but removing the problem has to be better than keeping it on display.

I'm willing my feet to move when the light blinds me again. Instead of looking away this time, I search the sky for its source. After two more hits, my eyes adjust to the brightness and I spot where it's coming from.

It's not the sun. It's Sam. He's controlling the lighting from inside a small white tent on top of a tall wooden platform behind the rows of chairs. And he's not trying to blind me — he's trying to get my attention. When he sees that I see him, he waves once and gives me a small smile.

I smile back. Somehow, knowing I have at least one friend in the crowd helps me regain focus. I glance at the girls — careful this time to ignore their looks, which are now all panicked — and immediately know where they are in the routine. As I jump in, I realize they're not as far along as I thought. The audience doesn't even seem to notice anything was wrong.

The rest of the routine goes perfectly. I don't miss another step or note, and my smile doesn't drop once. The other girls must perform just as well, because when the music stops and we freeze, the audience goes crazy. For a bunch of sophisticated, well-dressed professionals, they sure can make some noise. They cheer, whistle, and stomp their feet just like the whole town used to do at Curly Creek baseball games.

They're still yelling when the pink velvet curtain lowers. Once they're out of sight, we all jump out of our positions, squeal, and hug. I'm stunned when Ava throws her arms around my neck after doing the same to Megan, but I manage to hug her back.

The backstage area fills with people. Stagehands congratulate one another. Excited audience members congratulate us. Some excited audience members congratulate each other, and I assume these people are Constellation parents who'd like to take credit for creating such talent. I don't know anyone outside our little group, but I feel good—no, better than that. I feel great. I just sang and danced in front of eighty-four people, which is something I never would've done before. And now that I have, I can't wait to do it again.

"Excuse me?"

I turn when someone taps me on the shoulder. A young man holds a tape recorder toward me.

"I'm with the *Sweet Citrus Junior High Daily Squeeze*," he says. "How does it feel to be part of one of the hottest tween groups in Coconut Grove history?"

"Um—"

"Ruby, over here!" Megan yells.

"It feels amazing!" I call over my shoulder as I

run toward her and the rest of Constellation. They're huddled together near the backstage steps.

"You were fabulous," Mrs. Grand is saying as I join them. "Absolutely *fabulous*. The best you've ever been. And I can't wait for Luis Lobo to see you—and sign you—next week."

I laugh with the other girls. It seems impossible, but not so long ago, so did doing what we just did.

"On behalf of Ava's father and me, I'd like to present each of you with a very special gift." She reaches into a shopping bag behind her and pulls out a shoebox. "So that you'll feel like stars wherever you are."

"They're beautiful!" Megan gasps.

She's right. I never thought another pair of shoes could compare to my favorite red Converse . . . but these just might be the prettiest shoes I've ever seen. They're shiny gold sandals with long straps that, according to Ava's impromptu modeling session, wind up and tie around your calves. In the center of each, where the straps meet by the big toe, are glittery gold stars.

"I know you'll continue to make us proud," Mrs. Grand says before turning to talk to a reporter from the *Coconut Grove Gazette*.

The girls kick off their jazz shoes and dive into the shopping bag. I take my pair when Ava hands it to me, and then I dash down the backstage steps. I run down the center aisle of now-empty white chairs and hold the sandals in one hand as I use the other to climb up the ladder to the lighting tent.

"Thank you *so* much," I say breathlessly. "If I hadn't seen you when I did, I never would've—"

I stop when I reach the top of the ladder. The tent's empty. Sam's gone, and so is the equipment. It's like he was never there.

"Ruby."

I look down. Miss Anita is at the base of the ladder. Her assistant stands on tiptoe to keep the parasol above her head. After a second, she uses one finger to slowly slide her sunglasses down her nose.

I hook my arm over the top rung to keep from falling off.

Because Miss Anita's eyes are purple. Just like the ballerina in the painting.

I hold my breath and wait for her to say something. But she doesn't speak. She simply looks at me, slowly slides her sunglasses back into place, and glides away.

17. When Megan's mom drops me off at Nana Dottie's an hour later, I run inside as fast as my new gold sandals will carry me. I can't wait to tell Momma everything that just happened. I check the den, our bedroom, and the outside patio. Not finding her in any of her usual spots, I head for the kitchen. I smell something cooking, and I'm pretty sure that something's broccoli, which means Nana Dottie's at the stove. I hope Nana Dottie knows where Momma is—and will tell me without making me eat a field of vegetables first.

Because Momma and I always share big news over ice cream. I want to save my appetite for the triple-scoop hot fudge sundaes we'll have tonight.

I stop in the kitchen doorway. Three things seem off immediately.

1. Momma's in the kitchen. Cooking—
   not ordering takeout.
2. Nana Dottie's also in the kitchen.
   She's watching Momma cook.
3. They're both dressed like tennis players.

"Um . . . hi?" I say.

"Sweetie!" Momma looks up from a steaming pot and beams. "So glad you're home. I hope you're hungry."

I am . . . but for hot fudge sundaes. And the counter's currently covered in carrots and celery, not peanuts and sprinkles.

"Your mother is making a *feast*," Nana Dottie says. "I supplied the recipes, but she's done everything else herself."

"Wow." I step carefully into the kitchen, as if I might turn into a tennis-playing, health-food-eating clone the second my sandal hits tile. "That's great."

"Why don't you have a seat?" Momma turns back to the pot. "Dinner's almost ready. There's a pitcher of ice water and a bowl of fresh orange wedges on the drink cart. Help yourself!"

Ice water? Orange wedges? Where's the root beer? The fruit punch? The lemonade made from powder— not real lemons?

I'm still curious but less skeptical as I sit down and watch them. Something's up, but whatever it is, it's enabled them to be in the same room together without me there to chaperone. The progress is a little odd, but it's still progress.

"I'll get the music," Nana Dottie says a few minutes later. As she disappears into the living room, Momma carries a tray to the table.

"Fish?" My nose wrinkles before I can stop it.

"Salmon," Momma specifies, like that makes a difference. "Chock-full of healthy omega-3 fatty acids."

She says this like it's a good thing, but neither "fatty" nor "acid" sounds particularly good to me. I don't dwell on this for long, though, because something even stranger happens next.

Nana Dottie turns on classical music. And rather than cringing or covering her ears with her hands . . . Momma hums along.

"Are you okay?" I ask as she places a mountain of broccoli spears on the table.

"I am." She kisses the top of my head. "Today was a very good day, Ruby Lee."

I smile. She sounds happy, which is worth enduring fish and vegetables. Besides, I'll get the whole scoop over three scoops of chocolate ice cream later.

"Have you ever had anything more delicious than long-grain brown rice?" Nana Dottie asks when we're all seated. She closes her eyes and chews a forkful of brown mush. "It's like heaven on earth."

"How was your day, sweetie?" Momma asks before I can worry about how to answer that question. "Did rehearsal go well?"

"It did." Given the present situation, it feels like I sang and danced on Ava's stage days ago. "We ran through our routine for some of Mr. and Mrs. Grand's friends and colleagues."

"You didn't tell me you were doing that today," Momma says, sliding a piece of salmon onto my plate.

"That's because I didn't know about it until five minutes before it happened. But we actually did really well. We even got a standing ovation."

"Congratulations!" The spatula with a piece of pink fish freezes in midair as Momma stops serving to smile at me. "That's wonderful, Ruby."

"I knew it."

We both look at Nana Dottie, who's savoring another forkful of brown rice.

"It took a little while," she says, "but you're both fitting in. Everything's working out. I knew it would."

That makes one of us.

"How was your day?" I ask Momma eagerly. "What made it so good?"

"Well." She puts down the tray and shoots Nana

Dottie a quick smile. "First your grandmother and I got into a huge, noisy, record-breaking fight. It was so bad I made her pull the car over so I could get out and walk, but then it was so hot I got back in a minute later and we fought some more."

"Okay . . ." I glance at Nana Dottie. She looks happy too, so their record-breaking fight must not have caused permanent damage.

"*Then*," Momma continues, "I went on three interviews at three different salons. Now, at first I wanted to do something different from what I've always done, but I applied to twenty non-salon jobs in the past few weeks and was turned down for each and every one. After all that rejection, I thought it might be good to be back in a familiar environment. I also thought salon owners would welcome me with open arms and checkbooks, considering my extensive experience."

"Great idea," I say.

"I thought so." She takes three big gulps of ice water. "But the salon owners didn't agree."

"*What?* Did you tell them you were Employee of

the Month twenty-three times at the Curly Creek Nail Boutique? And that everyone loved talking to you even more than they loved getting manicures? And that Mrs. Jenkins cried when you told her we were moving?"

"I told them everything they needed to know." Momma pats my hand. "They said I just wasn't what they were looking for."

I sit back. "I really hope the day turned around after that."

"It sure did. Nana Dottie and I had organic salads for lunch—"

I make a face. I can't help it.

"—and then we went car shopping."

"You got a new car?" Now, *this* is good news. "What kind? Does it have air-conditioning? Automatic windows? A CD player? Is it outside? How did I miss it?"

I start to stand, but she squeezes my hand to stop me. "I didn't buy a new car. Even the used ones were too expensive. The salesman laughed when I told him my budget."

"Oh." I plop down. "No offense, Momma . . . but this sounds like the worst day ever."

"After that," she says, her smile growing, "Nana Dottie was late for her tennis game at the club. She didn't have time to drop me off at home and wouldn't let me drive the Jaguar, so I sat in the lobby and caught up on my knitting."

I relax slightly. Momma's been so busy looking for a job lately she hasn't had much time to knit. It was probably good for her to have a few hours to spend on that and nothing else. It didn't make up for the day before that point, but it was something.

"It was a great game, by the way," Nana Dottie chimes in. "And the conditions were perfect. Blue sky, low humidity."

"The humidity *was* low, wasn't it?" Momma agrees.

"Extremely," Nana Dottie says.

"Okay." I tap a fork against my water glass to get their attention. "Can we focus? Please?"

"Sorry." Momma turns to me. "You know how I do some of my best thinking while knitting?"

"Of course."

"Well, as I was working on a new tote bag, I remembered what your grandmother said about the club receptionist—the one who was going on maternity leave?"

"I remember." I also remember how mad Momma got when Nana Dottie suggested she be the temporary replacement.

"And sure enough, I looked up and there she was. Poor girl was as big as a house, but she was still working because they hadn't filled her position."

"They interviewed dozens of candidates," Nana Dottie says. "They just hadn't found anyone worth hiring."

I watch them exchange knowing looks. "And?"

"And I knitted two pairs of booties," Momma says, her voice triumphant. "One pink, one blue. Caroline just about passed out in her chair when I gave them to her."

That's it? One good deed and Momma's day went from miserable to magnificent?

"Your mother and Caroline got to talking," Nana Dottie explains. "They talked until I came to the lobby after my match. Your mom made such an impression,

Caroline immediately recommended her for the job."

"And I got it!" Momma squeals before I can process what Nana Dottie's saying. "I got the job—which means that in just a few weeks, I can go back to the dealer and bring home a new car!"

I'm thankful she's too excited to notice that my smile's forced. "That's amazing, Momma. Congratulations."

She misses my smile, but unfortunately, she catches my tone. "This is good news for both of us, Ruby. And like Nana Dottie said, the hours are perfect. I'll be home when you are."

"Perfect." I poke at my fish with my fork.

"Hey."

I look up. My stomach tightens when I see Momma's excitement replaced by concern.

"I get it," she says gently. "It's change, and change is hard. Especially when you have so much of it at once."

"I just didn't think you wanted that job. I'm a little surprised, that's all."

"It might not have been my first choice," Momma admits, "but that doesn't mean it won't still be great.

And when your grandmother mentioned it before, she was basically offering to use her connections to get me the position. That I definitely didn't want. Whatever job I got, I wanted to get it myself. On my own, fair and square. And I did."

I have to admit, this part makes sense. Momma didn't get the job because she filled out an application or gave them a fancy résumé—or because Nana Dottie asked the club to give it to her. She got the job because she knitted two pairs of booties for an overworked mother-to-be. She got it because she was herself.

"Wasn't there something else you wanted to tell Ruby?" Nana Dottie asks.

"There was." Momma jumps up, leaves the room, and comes back with a shopping bag. "Now, you know your grandmother and I don't always get along. We disagree about . . . well, pretty much everything. But she was right about me needing a job, and she was right about this job. It might've taken a while for me to realize it, but I did."

"Is that why we're having salmon, broccoli, and

long-grain brown rice for dinner? Because Nana Dottie might be right about junk food, too?" I turn to Nana Dottie. "No offense. It's delicious—it's just another surprise."

"Nana Dottie might've influenced the menu tonight," Momma says, "but I've wanted to start eating better for a long time. Old habits are hard to break, and I guess I was just waiting for the right time. And that's what this feels like."

I take the shopping bag when she hands it to me. I can't imagine what's inside and am almost nervous to open it. "An *iPod*?" I stare at the box, hardly believing it's real. "Momma, aren't these really expensive?"

"Whatever it cost was a small price to pay to see that smile." She sits down and refills our water glasses. "The only catch is that you put ABBA's greatest hits on there."

"Of course." I jump up and throw my arms around her. It's not just that she gave me a gift—it's that she seems to have accepted that sometimes going with the flow is easier than pushing against it. Which, I realize as I hug her, is exactly what she did by taking the job at the club. "Thank you."

"If you're lucky, next week I'll get you your very own Grove Club polo shirt." She straightens the collar of her new uniform and winks. "All the cool kids are going to want one."

We spend the next hour sitting around the table, eating, talking, and laughing. The salmon's better than I thought it would be, and I even have seconds. Between the Citrus Star performance preview, Momma's new job, and having dinner with Momma and Nana Dottie just like a regular family, this is easily the best day we've had since leaving Curly Creek.

And it only gets better.

"That's Oscar," Nana Dottie says when the doorbell rings. She gets up to answer it. "He's here for Scrabble night. You girls should join us."

Momma raises her eyebrows at me. I shrug.

"How hard can it be?" she asks.

Very, it turns out. Fortunately, neither Momma nor I care very much about our scores, and we spend more time laughing at the fake words we create than trying to come up with real ones. In fact, throughout the entire game, Momma plays only one word that can actually be found in the dictionary.

"I usually feel illiterate competing against your mother, but you make me feel like a genius," Oscar teases Momma after she puts down ZASPO for sixteen points. "Maybe I can thank you over dinner sometime?"

At which point Momma stares at the tiles on her tray, and Nana Dottie and I try to hide our smiles.

Momma's real word comes on her next turn. It's only three letters long but coincidentally earns her fifty points—the highest single score of the game.

YES.

18.

"Sorry!" I burst through the auditorium doors and fly down the aisle. "I'm *so* sorry I'm late. First Momma needed to stop for coffee, then we got stuck in traffic, then Mr. Fox and I couldn't figure out why I kept setting off the metal detectors . . ."

My voice trails off as I near the stage. I expected Ava, Stephanie, Hilary, and Megan to be in the middle of the routine by now, but they're sitting in a circle, not speaking. No one looks up as I approach, which must mean they're even more upset with me for being late than I thought they'd be.

"Did your gold sandals make the doors beep too?" I try to keep my voice casual, friendly.

"We didn't wear our gold sandals," Stephanie says.

"Thanks to you, we won't wear our gold sandals ever again," Hilary adds.

"What do you mean?" I stop in front of the stage and glance down at the sundress Momma and I bought at the mall yesterday. It's bright green instead of any of the light colors Ava and her friends usually wear, but it's still a sundress—and it looks great with the shiny shoes. If I made some kind of bad fashion statement that made them not want to be seen in their sandals, I have no idea what it is.

"Easy, girls," Ava says coolly. "It's not Ruby's fault that everything's ruined—oh, wait. Yes, it is."

I'm confused. We were all hugging and laughing the last time we were together. What could I have done to ruin everything since then? "I'm only fifteen minutes late. You're not even practicing yet."

Ava stands up slowly and walks to the front of the

circle. When she stops, her feet are inches away and level with my eyes. I don't want to look but can't help but see that she's not wearing gold sandals. She's not wearing black jazz shoes, either.

She's wearing red Converse.

"Of course we're not practicing. We had to wait for Constellation's brightest star."

My face is the same color as her sneakers when I meet her stare. "I'm sorry," I say again. "I know time's running out, and I really didn't mean to be late. But you could've started without me."

"Great idea! Why didn't I think of that?" Ava tilts her head like she's trying to figure out the answer to her question.

"Maybe because we didn't have a routine to start?" Hilary offers.

Ava snaps her fingers and lowers her eyes to mine. "Exactly."

They didn't have a routine? What happened to the one we've been rehearsing for nearly two months?

"Did someone try to steal our moves?" I ask,

suddenly remembering that this has been a problem in the past. "Do we have to change our routine?"

Ava's eyes narrow. "Yes."

Just thinking about learning a new routine is so exhausting I want to curl up in a ball and cry. "Can't we stop them? I mean, we already performed publicly. At least a hundred people know those moves are ours. Maybe we can talk to Miss Anita and—"

"I already talked to Miss Anita," Ava says.

"Oh." It's clear by her frown that the conversation didn't go well. "Ava, I promise I didn't say anything to anyone. I know things got off to a rocky start with us, but I would never betray the group. Ever."

"I'm very glad to hear that," Ava says. "Because you know how important Citrus Star is to us. You know how upset we'd be if we lost after working so hard for so long."

"I do." I nod. "And if we have to change the routine, I'll practice twenty-four hours a day until I get it right. I won't let you down."

The corners of her mouth lift in a small smile. "Then you better get started."

I turn away from the stage and dash to the first row of seats. I drop my stuff in a chair and bend down to undo the complicated sandal straps. As I kick them off and put on my jazz shoes, I wonder how I can convince Ava that if parts of our routine were stolen, I had nothing to do with it.

Thankfully, I have at least one ally.

"Megan?" I look up to see her hurriedly gathering her stuff five chairs down. "What are —"

"Can't talk," she says loudly.

I follow her glance up the center aisle. Ava, Stephanie, and Hilary are marching single file toward the auditorium doors.

"Wait for me," I say, scrambling for my backpack and sandals. "Where are we going?"

"You're not going anywhere," Megan practically yells.

I hear a door open and shut. Less than a second later, Megan's hand is on my arm.

"Ava's really mad, Ruby," she whispers.

"I figured." I hook my backpack on one shoulder and hug the sandals to my chest. "But why? What happened?"

She looks behind her. She's nervous. Scared, even. "Miss Anita was at the performance."

"I know. I didn't talk to her, but I got the impression that she liked what she saw."

"She did. A lot."

"So then what's the problem? And why do you look like you're worried the Phantom of Sweet Citrus Junior High is going to leap from the shadows and attack you?"

"I failed my last science test," she says, leaning closer. "It's my third F of the year. They might move me to a lower level—with the sixth graders."

For a second, this makes me forget my own problems. "Do you want to study together? I learned a lot of the material last year and would be happy to—"

"Megan Marie Hanley!" a voice bellows through the closed auditorium doors.

"I need her," Megan says, backing away and

shaking her head. "I'm sorry. She's my Oz, remember? Without her, I'd always be known as the girl without a brain — or friends."

"Megan, that's not true." I start after her, but she's already flying up the aisle. Knowing running after her will only make her run faster, I stop and watch her go. When she opens the auditorium door and lets in a panel of light, I realize she's wearing red Converse too.

"Ruby?"

I look up to see Sam leaning through a lighting booth window.

"Are you okay?" he asks.

"I don't know," I say truthfully. I feel like I've just been sucked up in a tornado, whipped about, and dropped in the middle of a cornfield. "I'm not sure what just happened."

He pauses. "My mom made blueberry coffee cake this morning. It's still warm. Do you want some?"

I consider the offer. There are about a million things I should do right now, starting with figuring out exactly what happened with our routine and how Ava expects me to fix it . . . but I nod anyway. Despite the million things I *should* do, eating warm blueberry coffee cake with Sam is what I *want* to do. At least for a few minutes.

As I climb the long, narrow staircase leading to the small booth overlooking the auditorium, I mentally replay the events of the last few days and try to pinpoint where I messed up. The only mistake I can think of is when I froze onstage in Ava's backyard and was late joining the routine. But the crowd didn't even notice my delay. They loved the performance—just like Miss Anita did. So if it's not that, then what is it?

"Holy electronics." I stop at the top of the stairs.

Sam looks around the booth, which is filled with big black boxes and long boards with flashing lights. "It looks more complicated than it is."

"I don't buy that for a second. Momma has a fit every time the oven light goes out because she never knows which bulb to buy."

"Why doesn't she write down the model number? Or take the old bulb with her when she goes to the hardware store?"

I raise my eyebrows. "You've obviously never met Momma."

"No. But I'd like to." He smiles, then looks down and fiddles with a knob on one of several control panels in the booth.

"Speaking of moms," I say quickly, since he seems embarrassed, "how about that blueberry coffee cake?"

"Coming right up!" He hops off the stool and removes a brown paper sack from the backpack at his feet. "I have to warn you: It's more cake than blueberry. Hope that's okay."

"I wouldn't have it any other way." I watch him break the thick, crumbly wedge into two pieces. "Do you bring your lunch to school a lot?"

"Every day." He carefully places my piece on a paper napkin and hands it to me. "I don't know if you've noticed . . . but I'm kind of shy."

"Really?" I definitely noticed the way he seems to magically appear and disappear, but since he's been so nice to me, I didn't pick up on the shyness. "So you bring your lunch so that you can hide behind the paper bag when necessary?"

"I bring my lunch so that I can avoid talking to people while waiting in line to buy lunch and while worrying about where to sit after that." He looks at me. "The cafeteria's a battlefield. I'm not a fighter."

"I bring my lunch every day, but I haven't actually eaten in the cafeteria once. I spend all period circling the room, pretending to look for friends I don't have. I eat after eighth period, when I'm waiting for Momma to pick me up."

"So you understand." He nods. "I had a feeling you would."

Now I'm embarrassed, though I'm not sure why. "Is that why you're doing the lighting for Citrus Star? To avoid singing and dancing in front of hundreds of people?"

"Exactly. Every year I present a ten-page plan to Miss Anita so she'll exempt me from performing. Fortunately, she finds the spotlight extremely important."

Considering the ballerina painting and wall of

mirrors in her office, this makes sense. "So how did you learn to do all this?" I ask, taking a big bite of coffee cake.

"I read a lot of books and watch a lot of movies and plays. Lighting affects everything from people's expressions to how they talk to the way an entire scene feels. I like experimenting with how I can make performers seem even more of whatever they're supposed to be — happy and excited, sad and lonely, mad and confused. It's interesting . . . and safe."

"Need an assistant?" I ask hopefully.

He smiles. "You're going to be great. I've been watching you — I mean, I've been watching Constellation, just like I've been watching every other group, since I'm doing the lighting for the whole show." He takes a breath. "Anyway, you're good. You're *really* good."

"That's sweet, Sam . . . but I don't have a talented bone in my body."

"Ruby Lee!"

We both jump. Unless Ava's anger has made her voice drop several octaves, I have no idea who's yelling for me. Sam looks out the window and leans to one side so I can see too.

"Hector," he says.

"Who's Hector?" I whisper, standing next to him. We're so close our arms gently bump together, and the touch almost makes me forget Ava, Constellation, and everything that happened only minutes earlier.

Apparently, the same thing happens to Sam, because it takes him a second to respond. And when he does, he doesn't use words—he switches on the spotlight and aims it toward the stage steps.

"Miss *Anita*?" I groan softly as she and her short male shadow walk across the stage. "What's she doing here?"

"You'll see," Sam says.

They stop in the center of the stage. She says something to him, and he shuffles backstage. I'm about to ask Sam what I'm supposed to see when he starts flicking switches and adjusting knobs on the control panel before us. The spotlight shuts off and the overhead lights dim until the auditorium is pitch black.

"Watch this," he says quietly.

I couldn't look away if I tried. The darkness only lasts a few seconds before the room fills with soft waves of light. They slowly flicker and spin across the walls, making the auditorium glow like it's underwater. Sam presses another button and another light turns on, this one still soft, but focused. He gets behind one of the big black boxes and aims the hazy ray at the stage, where a beautiful ballerina is standing perfectly still on the tips of her toes.

I'm so mesmerized by the swirling light and shadows that it takes me a moment to realize the beautiful ballerina is Miss Anita. She's wearing one of her long, flowing skirts, but she has removed a long, flowing top to reveal a white sleeveless leotard. She's looking down, and her dark hair hangs over one shoulder.

Sam holds the light in place with one hand and leans over to push a button with the other. Classical music, very similar to the kind Nana Dottie listens to, fills the room. It starts out soft, then gradually builds in volume. When the song explodes in a chorus of strings, Miss Anita's head snaps up. She leaps into the air—several feet higher than my best diving-board jump—and lands on the tips of her toes. She leaps again and again, her feet fluttering beneath her as she rises up and comes back down. The music grows quieter, slower, and she pirouettes around the stage, her skirt floating around her like a cloud. Sam follows her the entire time, moving the spotlight faster and slower depending on her movements. As she dances, soft waves of light continue to ripple across the walls, floor, and seats.

I'm not sure how long this lasts. As far as I'm concerned, we're no longer at school. Time no longer exists. We're suspended in some magical dimension filled with light and shadow, music and motion. I've never experienced anything like it.

Eventually, Miss Anita lands for the last time. She bends at the waist, and her torso drops toward her knees. The spotlight has illuminated her from head to toe during her performance, but now it narrows and focuses only on her face. She's not wearing sunglasses, and her purple-blue eyes are especially striking in the fuzzy light.

"She's beautiful," I breathe.

And then, as quickly as the performance began, the music ends and the main auditorium lights come on. When my eyes adjust, Miss Anita's wearing her long, flowing top and sunglasses, and she's standing next to Hector on the stage. They're both looking toward the lighting booth.

I look at Sam.

"I'm right here if you need me," he says.

Given his fear of people and confrontation, this probably shouldn't be reassuring. But it's enough to get me moving downstairs. Plus, as much as I'd like to, it's not like I can hide out here forever.

"Good morning, Miss Anita," I say as I near the stage. "That was an incredible —"

"Ruby," she says, "do you know what Sirius is?"

I reach the stage and stop. "Sure do. It's what I am about Citrus Star. It's what I am about making sure Constellation's performance is as good as it can possibly be."

She sighs, and I know her eyes roll behind her sunglasses. "Not *serious*. Sirius. S-i-r-i-u-s."

I visualize the letters as she spells them. "The brightest star in the solar system?"

Hector gives her a quick smile. He, for one, is impressed. Wait till he finds out what I know about Pluto.

"That's what you are," she says.

Any satisfaction I feel instantly disappears. "I'm sorry?"

"Ava Grand is good. But you, Ruby. *You* are great."

I sneak a peek at the booth, hoping Sam can shed some light on this cryptic conversation.

"I know raw talent when I see it, and I saw it in you at your performance preview."

"You mean when I froze onstage? And stood like a statue while everyone else sang and danced? *That* performance preview?"

"You lack confidence," Miss Anita says. "That comes with practice. The rest you already have."

"I'm sorry," I say again, shaking my head. "I don't understand. Are you—"

"Ava's out."

My chin hits my neck.

"Not completely. She'll still sing and dance backup. But you will be Constellation's soloist."

"No way. I mean, thank you so much for the compliment, but—"

"This isn't a compliment. It's the truth."

"Either way, Citrus Star is three days away. I don't know Ava's part. I don't know if I can hit those big notes."

"You can't," Miss Anita says flatly. "At least not yet. That's why you should pick a different song. One you already know, one that you're emotionally connected to. I've instructed the rest of the group to do as you say."

"And if they don't?" I ask, trying not to panic and failing miserably.

She lowers her head. Purple-blue slivers appear above her sunglasses. "That's not your concern."

It's by far my *biggest* concern, but before I can tell Miss Anita that, she starts moving across the stage. My panic eases slightly as I watch her go . . . because she's limping. She usually glides everywhere, but now her movements are awkward, stilted. She favors her left foot and jerks to the right. When she reaches the steps, she waits for Hector. He gently puts one arm under her legs and the other behind her back, and he carries her off the stage.

I wait until the auditorium door closes behind them before looking up at the lighting booth.

"She's right," Sam says apologetically.

Which is no help whatsoever.

19.

Beyoncé, Fergie, Lady Gaga, Shakira, Pink. Who *are* these people?"

"Deep breath," Gabby says on the other end of the phone.

"I've downloaded twenty of the top one hundred songs on iTunes. I've played each song a million times. I've found lyrics online, printed them out, and tried singing along. I've spent eleven hours watching videos and studying dance moves on MTV." I stop pacing and drop onto a white leather couch. "And now I'm forty-eight hours away from being laughed all the way back to Kansas."

"Perfect! The Curly Creek Country Fair is this weekend. You'll get here just in time for hay rides and caramel apples."

"I love the Curly Creek Country Fair," I whimper, collapsing back into the couch cushions and covering my face with a pillow.

"Okay, seriously, didn't crazy ballerina lady tell you to sing something you already know? And that you're emotionally connected to? Wouldn't that be easier than trying to learn a song you've never heard before?"

"Yes, except there are only two people at Sweet Citrus Junior High who listen to the same music I do. One's a seventy-year-old security guard, and the other probably will never speak to me again if I ask Ava Grand to do something she doesn't want to do. My only hope of surviving this is singing a song everyone already knows and likes."

"If you say so," Gabby says doubtfully. "But whichever one you pick, just remember that crazy ballerina lady wouldn't have made you the soloist if she didn't think you could do it."

"Right. I'll be sure to send her a thank-you card."

"Better make it an e-mail."

I sit up on the couch when the front door opens and closes. Momma comes into the living room and kisses the top of my head, then drops into a nearby chair, closes her eyes, and starts rubbing her temples. When the clicking of Nana Dottie's high heels across the marble floor heads in our direction, Momma winces.

"Um, Gabby . . . I have to go. I'll call you later." We say good-bye and hang up. "Momma? Are you all right?"

"Ruby," she says with a sigh, "if we ever win the lottery and have bazillions of dollars to spend however we want . . . let's not join a country club."

"Okay."

She opens her eyes and looks at me. "Seriously. Promise me that even after we've bought a house, a car, and more clothes than we'll ever wear and we still have bazillions left over, that you will not let me spend even one penny on anything in, near, or related to a country club."

"I promise."

"Thank you, sweetie." She gives me a small smile, then closes her eyes again.

"It's not really fair to blame the club, Francine," Nana Dottie says, entering the room and sitting next to me.

Even from five feet away, I can see Momma's whole body tense. "Blame the club for what?" I ask.

"Nothing," Momma says. "There was a teeny tiny accident at work today, but everything's fine now."

"Fine?" Nana Dottie says. "The club had to close. They're not sure when it will reopen. You call that *fine*?"

"So a bunch of superrich people will have to entertain themselves with activities that don't involve hitting small balls into holes and over nets. They're superrich. They'll find something."

I look at Nana Dottie. She looks at Momma.

"Francine—"

"It was an *accident*, Mom," Momma says, sitting up. "I told you I don't want to talk about it."

"And I told you we're *going* to talk about it. We spent so many years not talking when we should have, and where did that get us? But you and Ruby are here now. We're family. And we're going to discuss things when they need to be discussed."

I start to stand, prepared to excuse myself and let them talk privately, but Nana Dottie presses down on my shoulder until I'm seated again.

"I did exactly what I was asked to do," Momma says, her voice low. "They asked me to flip a switch and reboot the computer system. That's what I did."

"They said rebooting the computer system was as *easy* as flipping a switch. You weren't supposed to literally flip a switch."

"Well, how was I supposed to know that?" Momma bursts. "I've spent as much time on computers as I have eating tofu. I have no idea how they work."

"Then you should've *asked*," Nana Dottie says. "And if there was no one there you felt comfortable approaching, you should've called me. I would've talked you through it."

"I'm thirty-two years old. I'm an adult. I've never had my mother's help before, and I don't need it now."

Nana Dottie pauses, clearly taken aback by Momma's words. When she speaks again, her voice is firmer. "You'd rather pull the plug on the entire club, plunging guests into darkness and costing the owners thousands of dollars? That's the better option?"

Momma frowns. "No one was hurt, and I'm sure the club will survive the financial setback."

"Today's, yes. But what about tomorrow's? And the next day's? Whatever you did, it not only cut off the normal power supply, but it fried the generators. There's no telling when everything will be up and running again. And until it is, employees still have to be paid, members have to be reimbursed, additional income from the restaurant and public golf course will be lost. All because you were too stubborn to ask for help."

"I have some money," I say quickly. "From babysitting in Curly Creek. It's not much, but it's something."

"That's a lovely offer, Ruby," Momma says, "but we don't have to pay back the club. It was an accident. Accidents happen all the time."

"This kind doesn't."

I turn to Nana Dottie. Her bright pink lips press together, and her thin black eyebrows lift. She looks more serious now than she did when she first entered the room, which makes me think we haven't heard the worst of it yet.

Unfortunately, I'm right.

"Given the severity of the situation and your brief period of employment," Nana Dottie continues, "the owners feel that action must be taken."

"Action?" Momma's voice is softer now . . . timid, even. "What kind of action?"

"They can't fire her," I say, resisting the urge to run to Momma and give her a big hug. "Can they?"

Nana Dottie looks down at her hands, which are clasped in her lap. "I'm afraid they can."

Momma gasps, then releases a light, nervous laugh. "But they won't. I'm your daughter. You're their friend — and a responsible, dues-paying member. They wouldn't want to upset you like that."

"We've already spoken. They said you have two choices: You could repay every dollar your technological mishap cost them, or you can leave. For good."

"They talked to you before talking to me? What kind of—"

"I offered to cover the cost." Nana Dottie's eyes lock on Momma's. "Every last dime, no matter the amount. I wanted to save you the stress of finding another job."

Momma sits back. Her shoulders slump. She looks tired, defeated, completely unlike herself. "Thank you. That was very generous."

"Yes. Well." Nana Dottie pauses. "I've changed my mind."

Momma's mouth opens, but nothing comes out.

"You're thirty-two years old. You're an adult. If you don't need my help, fine. I won't force you to accept it. You're on your own."

And with that, Nana Dottie stands up and leaves the room.

I look at Momma. She's staring at the empty spot next to me, like Nana Dottie's still on the couch. Her mouth hangs open. She doesn't blink. I'm about to ask if there's anything I can do when her chin shoots up and her head snaps toward me.

"Get your things," she says before jumping up and disappearing down the hallway.

I hurry after her. By the time I reach the bedroom, she's already pulled our old duffel bags from the closet and started stuffing them with clothes. She moves quickly, yanking drawers open, shoving them shut, grabbing bottles of hairspray and lotion and tossing them toward the bags on the bed.

"Pack," she says without looking at me. "Grab your clothes, camera, laptop, iPod—whatever you can carry."

"Are we going somewhere?" I'm not sure whether to be hopeful or nervous. On the one hand, with Citrus Star only two days away, I barely have time for bathroom breaks. On the other hand, if I can't make Citrus Star because of some sort of family emergency, that wouldn't be the worst thing in the world.

"I picked up a bus schedule weeks ago, just in case we ever needed it. The next one leaves in fifteen minutes."

Momma gathers shoes from the closet floor. "We have to hurry."

"Are we going to Disney World?" My heart races at the thought of a vacation.

"Even better." Momma drops an armful of shoes on the bed, stands before me, and takes my face in her hands. "We're going home."

She releases my face and my chin falls. "*Home*, home?" I ask.

"The only one we have."

I stand there, my thoughts spinning like a tornado has somehow wiggled through one ear and into my head. I don't have to be in Citrus Star. I don't have to mortify myself in front of a thousand strangers. I don't have to go back to Sweet Citrus Junior High. I don't have to wear sundresses or metallic sandals. I don't have to see Ava Grand ever again.

There's just one problem.

"What about Nana Dottie?"

"What about her?" Momma zips up the duffel bags and slings them onto her shoulders.

"I know you just had a little fight, but—"

"A little fight?" Momma faces me. "Ruby, I hope you and your grandmother have a nice relationship one day. Truly, I do. But my mother and I will never be close. I hoped we could be—even though she left me years ago for a fancy house, a fancy car, and a fancy life she thought she'd never have in Curly Creek. I hoped that our moving here was a chance to start over and make things better. But I was wrong. Our relationship is too broken to fix."

I know Momma and Nana Dottie don't always get along, but after everything that's happened in the past few months, it doesn't feel right to just up and leave. Unfortunately, Momma's determined to make the next bus out of Coconut Grove; she's heading down the hallway before I can suggest taking a later one after talking to Nana Dottie.

I quickly gather my stuff and fly from the bedroom to the family room. As Momma collects her knitting supplies, I turn on my laptop and connect to the Internet. I've just started an e-mail to Megan and Sam when

Nana Dottie appears in the doorway. She's holding a plastic-wrapped package in one hand and a zucchini in the other.

"I'm making swordfish and steamed vegetables for dinner," she says, her voice even. "Will you be joining me?"

My excitement knots in my stomach. During the countless times I'd imagined going home over the past few months, I felt like I couldn't leave Coconut Grove fast enough. But now that my dream is on the brink of reality, leaving isn't so easy. Nana Dottie hasn't talked much about Papa Harry, but she must still miss him. What if losing us makes her feel even worse about losing him? What if she's lonely?

"Francine?" Nana Dottie says when Momma continues to gather her knitting supplies without answering. "What are you doing?"

"We're leaving," I say when Momma doesn't answer. I didn't imagine this part, either. I always thought Momma would sit Nana Dottie down for a nice, calm conversation well in advance of our departure. "We're going home."

"Home? What do you . . . ?" Nana Dottie's voice trails off as her eyes land on Momma's duffel bag.

"You said we had two choices," Momma says. "We could pay for everything we damaged, or we could leave. So we're leaving."

"Oh, for heaven's sake, Francine. No one meant for you to leave the *state*. Now, put down your things and have a seat. I'll make some tea and we'll talk this through."

"*No.*" Momma grabs one last ball of yarn, stands up straight, and looks at Nana Dottie. "No more talking. Ruby and I are going home. It was a mistake to come here, and now we're going to get our life back on track. Our bus leaves in twelve minutes."

I glance at Nana Dottie. Her mouth opens and closes like she has so much and nothing to say at the same time.

"Go," she finally manages.

"Nana Dottie," I say, stepping toward her, "I—"

"Outside. Now." She gives me, then Momma, a stern look.

We were already leaving, but getting kicked out

throws even Momma. Her face softens for the first time since she walked in the door.

"Do you have any idea how many germs are on those buses? It's a miracle they haven't been condemned." Nana Dottie opens the front closet and removes her purse. "I'll drive you."

"You'll *what*?" Momma shakes her head like she didn't hear right. "Mom . . . Kansas is two thousand miles away. You haven't driven farther than the Super Walmart in twenty years."

"I'll stop twice an hour for bathroom and junk food breaks."

Momma looks at me. I shrug. "Can we eat in the car?" she asks.

Thirty seconds later, we're standing on the front stoop, waiting for the garage door to open. Momma stares at a palm tree, not speaking. I want to ask if she's okay, but since I think I already know the answer to that, I distract myself with my camera. I take pictures of the yard, the pink house next door, and our old dead hatchback parked on the street. I suddenly want to remember everything about the place we tried to call home for a few months, and I take so many pictures I finish one roll of film and have to load another.

I've just closed the camera when the garage door opens . . . and Papa Harry's yellow convertible backs out.

"Well?" Nana Dottie calls out when Momma and I don't move from the stoop. "Are we going, or what?"

Momma looks at me. "Shotgun."

"Please keep the interior clean," Nana Dottie says as we hurry to the car and climb in. "You may eat in here, but you may not engage in food fights or any other activity that might harm the leather seats. Are we clear?"

"Crystal," Momma says.

"And don't ask me to put the top down. There's a five percent chance that it might rain later, and that's a chance I'm not willing to take."

Surprisingly, the convertible's interior and top are Nana Dottie's only sticking points. For the next three hours, she lets us do whatever we want. She lets Momma blast oldies on the radio and doesn't bat an eye when we both sing along at the top of our lungs. She doesn't say anything when we roll down our windows and wave good-bye to some of our favorite landmarks from our drive down, like the country's biggest Cracker Barrel restaurant, the coffee shop shaped like a coffee bean, and the giant sign announcing Alvin's Alligator Farm and Casino. And she exits the highway twice an hour for bathroom breaks and junk food, just like she said she would. She even tries beef jerky at Momma's insistence—and likes it.

Riding in Papa Harry's car with Momma and Nana Dottie is probably the most fun I've had since leaving Curly Creek. It's just too bad we didn't do it sooner.

The good times continue through the fourth hour. In the fifth, the rain starts. Softly at first, and then harder and harder, until it's falling in thick sheets around us and pounding the car so aggressively I worry the top will buckle under the beating. Nana Dottie's been cruising at a good clip until this point, but she slows to a crawl when the sky opens up.

"You've been driving for hours," Momma shouts

over the rain as a shard of lightning rips through the blackness in front of us. "Why don't I take a turn so you can rest?"

"I don't need to rest." Nana Dottie's fingers tighten around the steering wheel. "I feel fine."

It's eleven o'clock at night. I've eaten more Doritos, cookies, and Milky Ways than most kids eat in a month. I'm exhausted, I'm full, and I wish I were sleeping . . . especially since the fun is about to come to a grinding halt.

"Mom," Momma tries again when thunder booms overhead and the car jerks to the left. "It's pitch black. If you don't want me to drive, will you at least pull over until the storm passes?"

"I don't need to pull over," Nana Dottie says. "You want to go home, and I'm going to get you there."

"And you will." Momma glances in the backseat, and I know she's making sure I'm wearing my seat belt. "But there's no rush. We'll get there when we get there."

Nana Dottie doesn't respond—or if she does, I don't hear her. The wind's picking up now, and it grows from a whisper to a roar. It nudges the car from side to side. I peer through the window and see road signs flapping and branches flying from trees.

"This isn't good," I say, even though no one can hear me.

"I didn't leave you," Nana Dottie shouts.

"What?" Momma shouts back.

"Years ago, when I met Harold and we decided to leave Curly Creek. I didn't leave *you*."

I watch Momma watch Nana Dottie. Her eyes are wide and her mouth's open, like she can't believe Nana Dottie has chosen this moment to finally say what has needed to be said for decades.

"I asked you to come," Nana Dottie continues, her fingers gripping the steering wheel so tightly I think it might crack. "I begged you to. For years I tried to get you to join us. You wouldn't do it."

"I was eighteen. I had friends in Curly Creek. I had a life. You knew I didn't want to leave—and you left anyway. You had a choice, and you chose a fancy new life over the one you already had."

Another bolt of lightning tears through the sky. It lights up the car, and I see Momma leaning forward in her seat, looking at Nana Dottie. I'm pretty sure they've both forgotten about the storm raging outside, which makes me squeeze the door handle even tighter.

"Harold was a kind, decent, caring man," Nana Dottie fires back. "He would've done anything for you if you'd given him a chance."

"I tried," Momma says. "When Ruby was born. I invited you both back to spend time with us, and you didn't come."

"We were busy—"

"You were at a business convention!" Momma declares. "In sunny Puerto Rico! You had another chance, and you made the same choice!"

"That convention had been planned for months! I asked if we could come two weeks later, and you said no. And you never invited us back. I might never have met Ruby until you moved here if I hadn't surprised you with a visit five years ago."

"Um, guys?" I shout when a gust of wind shoves the

car to the right, over the double yellow line and into the next lane. "It's pretty bad out there; maybe we should—"

"It hurt too much," Momma says, ignoring me. "Okay? Are you happy? I was so excited to spend time with you both, and I was crushed when you didn't come. It hurt as much as it did the day you left, when I was eighteen, and I didn't want to feel anything like that ever again."

Nana Dottie's head snaps toward Momma. "You think knowing you're hurt makes me happy? Nothing could be further from the truth! And I missed you, too. So much. My heart ached every single day."

"Then why didn't you come back? Why didn't you tell Harry that you wanted to be with us and come back for good?"

"You stopped talking to me. I didn't think you wanted to see me."

I stare at Nana Dottie's trembling shoulders. Now's really not a good time for an emotional breakdown.

"I called you," Nana Dottie continues. "I wrote. I invited you to visit. And when you ignored me, I just longed for the day when we would mend our relationship and begin healing as a family."

"Well, I guess that day hasn't come yet, has it?" Momma shouts as six lightning bolts zoom toward the ground. They're so close I think I could reach out and touch them.

"I won't disappoint you again, Francine," Nana Dottie shouts back. "I know living together hasn't been easy, and I wish you would stay so we could work it out, but if you don't want to, I'm not going to stop you. I'm going to bring you home if it's the last—"

"Look out!" I scream as two metal garbage cans fly at the windshield.

The car veers sharply to the left. It spins slowly, then seems to lift off the ground and float through the air. When it hits the pavement again, it takes three more tight, fast spins before sliding across the shoulder and landing in a shallow ditch.

"Ruby!" Momma yells once the car stops. She unbuckles and twists frantically in her seat. "Oh my goodness, Ruby, sweetie, are you okay?"

"Give her a second." Nana Dottie's voice is calm as she presses one hand to mine.

My eyelids feel weighted down with bricks when I try to open them. They finally lift on my third attempt, and at first, I think I'm dreaming. I must have a concussion or be in a coma.

Because I don't see Momma and Nana Dottie inside Papa Harry's car. I see them planting flowers in the backyard. Talking in the living room. Playing Scrabble. I see Nana Dottie doing her crossword puzzle and listening to classical music. I see Momma surrounded by balls of yarn and jumping into the pool in her grass skirt and coconut bra. I see other people, too. Mr. Fox holding my lunch box. Megan listening to her Walkman. Ava dancing in her bedroom. Miss Anita gliding down the hallway. Sam grinning in the lighting booth. Oscar dancing by the pond in his flower shop.

And then I see sunflowers. Hundreds of big, bright, happy yellow sunflowers. They're swaying together in a field and seem to be waving to me.

"Momma?" I whisper.

"I'm right here, sweetie." She squeezes my hand. "What is it?"

"Are we in Kansas?"

There's a pause. "No, honey. Not yet."

Somehow, my mouth lifts in a small smile. "Then can we go home? To Coconut Grove?"

20.

"I don't think I can do this."

I take Megan's hand and gently pull her away from the velvet curtain.

"There are a million people out there," she says, fanning her face with a thin stack of paper. "That's a million more than I've played for in my entire life."

"What about your parents?" I ask. "You must've played for them."

"So they could tell me how terrible I am and suggest I try another hobby, like napping or staring at the wall?" She shakes her head. "I don't think so."

We both turn when a high-pitched giggle cracks through the hum of kids around us singing scales, shuffling through dance moves, and whispering about the competition. Ava's perched on a small table as Stephanie laces her shoes and Hilary freshens her makeup. They all wear the costume Ava's personal designer created weeks before: a sleeveless leotard, short tutu, and leg warmers made of silk instead of wool that end above the knee instead of midcalf. The only difference between the costumes is that Stephanie's and Hilary's are white, while Ava's is red. Also, Ava looks like she showered in glitter and forgot to towel off. She sparkles from head to toe, which makes the others blend in with the background even more.

"She probably broke the piano," Megan whispers. "She probably cut the strings inside so that when I sit down and play in front of a million people, all they hear are the keys clunking down."

"No offense," I say, watching Ava purse her lips so Hilary can reapply her lipstick, "but I don't think she considers us—or anyone else—competition. She wouldn't waste her precious time sabotaging what didn't need to be sabotaged."

"You're not dressed."

We turn back to find Miss Anita and Hector standing behind us.

"Citrus Star begins in four minutes." Miss Anita peers down at us through her sunglasses. "And you're wearing a tablecloth and jeans while the rest of your group is wearing leotards and tutus."

I glance down at my shirt, which, with its blue-and-white-checked print does kind of resemble something you'd put your dinner on, and then look at Miss Anita. "You said Constellation should do what I asked them to."

Miss Anita's red lips curve down. "You asked them to look like professional dancers while you looked like a professional farmer?"

I'm glad the backstage lights are dim so she can't see my face turn pink. "Sort of. There's a little more to it than that."

She steps toward me. Hector steps next to her. He looks nervous.

"I did make it clear that this was an opportunity, yes? Perhaps the biggest one of your life?"

She doesn't sound pleased, but for some reason, being reminded that this is an opportunity makes me feel braver. "You did. And I won't waste it. I promise."

She pauses, as if trying to decide whether to believe me. "I certainly hope not."

"She's going to kill us," Megan moans when Miss Anita glides away, her bright orange skirt floating behind her. "If I don't die of stage fright first, I'm going to die by Miss Anita's evil stare."

"She's not evil," I say, peeking through the curtain at the inside of the Coconut Grove Theater. It's as crowded as Nana Dottie said it would be; every seat's taken and dozens of people stand in the back. "She's sad. And in a way, she's generous. She wants for others what she didn't have for herself."

"A lifetime of embarrassment jam-packed into four short minutes?"

That's not quite it, but the explanation will have to wait. Sam's story of how Miss Anita broke her leg during her debut performance with the New York City Ballet and never danced professionally again took half an hour. I expect Megan to have just as many questions as I did, and right now, we don't have that kind of time.

"They're dimming the lights," she whispers, grabbing my arm.

The other groups rush toward the curtain as Miss Anita takes center stage. We all clamor for a closer look at our audience—which is now invisible, thanks to the lowered main lights and the spotlight shining on Miss Anita. Her bright orange dress glows and floats in the shifting auditorium air, and I think we could crown her Citrus Star now and call it a day.

But then, of course, all of our hard work will have been for nothing. It took a while to convince Momma I felt fine after Papa Harry's car landed in the ditch by the field of sunflowers, but once I did, I slept for ten hours: five during the drive back to Coconut Grove and five in my comfy bed. As soon as I woke up, I started e-mailing.

I e-mailed Megan and Sam, told them my idea, and

asked if they'd be willing to participate. When they said they would, I e-mailed Ava and told her that due to unforeseen circumstances, Megan and I were respectfully bowing out of Constellation and wished her luck. Then I e-mailed Megan and Sam again and the real planning began. Unfortunately, time restraints made it impossible to put all the pieces together at once for a real run-through, but I wasn't too worried. Sam knew his stuff, and despite what she thought, Megan knew hers, too. I wasn't as sure about myself, but at that point, I thought I had nothing to lose.

"Good evening."

I'm snapped back to the present when Miss Anita speaks into the microphone.

"Thank you for joining us for a thrilling evening of singing, dancing, and general stardom. As I'm sure you know, your talented children have been preparing tirelessly for tonight's performance. And with very good reason. Previous winners of Citrus Star have gone on to see their dreams realized onstage and screen, from Disney World to the Disney Channel. One has even become a popular recording artist with a top twenty hit in Hong Kong." She waits as the audience buzzes appreciatively. After a moment, she continues. "These children are stars. I know it. You know it. And after tonight, the whole world may know it too. So please sit back, relax, and enjoy the show."

The room goes black. My heart jumps. For a second, I think Sam is experiencing technical difficulties in the lighting booth, but then a row of orange bulbs lining the front of the stage flickers on. Music starts.

And Citrus Star begins.

There's a flurry of activity backstage as groups squeeze in last-chance practices before their turns. Coincidentally, the only kids *not* running through routines are current and former Constellation members. Ava, Stephanie, and Hilary hang out near the restroom. Stephanie and Hilary seem tense, like they wouldn't mind giving the routine another go, but Ava leans against the wall looking per- fectly relaxed—and almost bored. It's clear she thinks she's already won, which she probably has.

As for Megan and me, there's not much we can do

now. Every few minutes she looks at the papers in her hand, but without a piano, that's not very helpful. And I'm not about to practice my part and alert anyone to our plan.

The first group opens the show with a bang — literally. There's a small explosion that sends thick white smoke billowing across the stage. As it thins and spreads, three boys appear like ghosts rising from the ground. I recognize them from my English class, though it takes me a second, since they're wearing shiny black basketball shorts and baggy black tank tops instead of jeans and T-shirts. They leap and flip across the stage and seem to be playing some acrobatic version of basketball minus the actual ball and hoops. I'm so entranced I don't realize the crowd's roaring until the curtain closes and they jog backstage.

"We don't have explosions," Megan whispers. "Or smoke."

"We don't need them," I assure her.

The next group juggles flaming batons. The one after that plays, on electric guitars, one of the songs I downloaded from iTunes. The one after that reenacts a scene from *Hannah Montana*, which Megan informs me is a TV show about a regular girl who's also a rock star. On and on they go, singing, dancing, hopping, skipping, cartwheeling. Each performance makes the crowd howl even louder than the one before, but personally, I don't see the big deal. The kids are good. Some of them are really good. But besides Sam's supreme lighting skills and the occasional pyrotechnic display, Citrus Star doesn't seem all that different from a Curly Creek talent show.

Until Ava Grand takes the stage.

"She looks amazing," Megan says softly, peering through the curtain.

It's true. She does. And as the music begins and the curtain rises, I feel nervous for the first time since the show started. The audience seems to feel the same way; they grow quiet and still, like they know something important is about to happen.

Constellation doesn't disappoint. The routine hasn't changed since we performed it at Ava's house only days before, but somehow it looks different. I'm not sure if it's the costumes, Sam's magical lighting, or the combination of both, but the effect is bigger. More dramatic. Dance moves that seemed robotic a few weeks ago are now strong, purposeful. The singing is flawless. Stephanie and Hilary harmonize like they never have before, and Ava belts out notes like Celine Dion (another of Momma's favorites who no one here seems to know). They're a million times better than anything I watched on MTV. In fact, they should probably have their own channel: CTV. Constellation Television. Nothing but Ava, Stephanie, and Hilary, 24/7.

Not surprisingly, the crowd goes nuts. They scream and whistle. They jump to their feet and clap so fast their hands blur white. They throw things onstage—roses, teddy bears, tiaras—and demand an encore. And I don't blame them. I'm clapping too. Ava might have given me a hard time for no reason, but she worked extremely hard to make sure Constellation put on a good show. She and the other girls deserve all the accolades they get.

"Great job," I say when they dash past us backstage.

Ava stops short and looks at me over her shoulder. "Nice shirt."

They return to their post by the restroom and fix their hair and costumes. They're getting ready to give an encore . . . and after Ava's last comment, I don't even worry about how mad they'll be when they don't get the chance.

"Ladies and gentlemen." A familiar male voice booms down from above. "I hope you enjoyed that stellar performance by Constellation. Those girls are definitely ones to watch out for."

I look at Megan. Her face is pale and she's sweating like the auditorium vents are spewing hot air instead of cold. I put one arm around her shoulders and squeeze.

"Now, I know your programs indicate that theirs was the final performance of the evening, but I'm very happy to announce that the show's not over yet."

Ava, Stephanie, and Hilary trot back to the curtain. They exchange confused looks, since encores don't usually require reintroductions, but then they smile as they prepare to face their fans for a second time.

"We had a late addition," Sam continues. "And I hope you'll join me in giving a very warm, very Coconut Grove welcome to . . . Pluto."

"What?" Ava glares at me with wide eyes and then storms off, most likely in search of Miss Anita. Stephanie and Hilary shoot me similar looks before racing after her.

"I can't do this. I can't do this. I can't do this." Megan stares through a narrow opening in the curtain and shakes her head.

There's no place like home. There's no place like home. There's no place like home.

"Yes, you can." I gently turn her away from the curtain and put both hands on her shoulders. "You're brilliant. No one in this school can do what you've done and what you're about to do."

"I don't know, Ruby," she says as the audience takes their seats and grows quieter. "Maybe this is a bad idea. What if they laugh? What if they never talk to me again?"

"Then it's their loss." I hold her eyes with mine.

When I speak again, my voice is softer. "You don't need her, Megan. You don't need anyone but yourself."

I hold my breath. She still doesn't seem sure, but finally she nods. We hug quickly, and she steps out from behind the curtain.

My heart races as I watch her sit on the piano bench and arrange the sheet music before her. The auditorium lights dim until the only light in the room comes from a tiny lamp attached to the top of the music stand. It's just bright enough to illuminate Megan's blue-and-white-checked shirt and her two long braids tied with blue ribbons. Because you can't see her hands, you don't realize right away where the music's coming from.

Which is almost too bad. Because she's as good as I knew she would be.

The song starts softly, simply. A few notes, like coins dropping in a glass jar. As they fill the room, a wide screen lowers behind the piano. Another follows, and another, and another. They're all different sizes and hang at various heights. When they stop moving they glow gray, reminding me of a window display at Curly Creek TVs and Toasters.

Black-and-white images appear. A small house. A large field. An apple tree. An old car with stuffed garbage bags for windows. Two hands, clasped in the grass.

The song is "Somewhere Over the Rainbow." The pictures are ones I took right before leaving Curly Creek.

Together, they're my cue.

I close my eyes and take a deep breath. I see the images in my head and focus on the music. When I step out onto the stage, I imagine I'm in our old living room in Curly Creek and that the only one watching me is Momma.

I move slowly at first. My arms and legs are relaxed as I twirl toward the audience and smile. This part of the dance is natural and easy, just like hanging out at home on an ordinary day.

But then Megan's fingers move faster. The music gets louder. My body tenses as a small black ball with a million bulbs spins overhead, sending waves of light rippling across the walls. I zigzag across the stage, my movements sharp, almost frantic. Pictures tremble and jump from one screen to the next. The lights grow brighter. My feet move faster. Soon it's so bright everything disappears.

And then the music stops. The lights go out. I collapse to the stage.

It's dark when Megan starts playing again. The music has changed. It's not "Somewhere Over the Rainbow" or any other song from *The Wizard of Oz*—though it does sound like something from a movie. Megan's fingers hit so many notes at once it's hard to believe she's only playing one instrument, and they do so with feeling. Not only did she write the music for this part of the performance, she knows how to play it in a way that everyone can connect to, even without ever hearing it before.

As the song grows, so do the lights. The stage is bathed in a soft, warm glow. I sit up slowly and watch the screens come to life again. They fill with images of palm trees and orange groves. These pictures are yellow and cream, and they look almost hazy, like they've been left out in the sun too long.

Eventually, I stand up and stretch, as if waking from a long nap. I twirl and leap from one picture to the next, pausing before each one and looking at it as if seeing it for the first time.

I move faster as the music picks up again. The soft, warm glow fades as spotlights illuminate individual screens. The audience gasps and whispers as they recognize people and places. There's Sweet Citrus Junior High. The Lemon Grove Mall. HauteCoco. The Atlantic Ocean. Mr. Fox. Mr. Soto. Miss Anita. Hector. Me. Megan. Sam. Ava. Stephanie. Hilary. Kids I don't know by name walking down the hall, playing soccer outside, talking and laughing in the cafeteria. The screens are alive with color as the pictures radiate red, yellow, orange, blue, green, and purple. The music is bright and happy, and my smile grows as my arms and legs follow the beat.

Between the pictures, Megan's song, Sam's lighting, and my dancing (I hope), Coconut Grove looks like a magical place somewhere far, far away.

Eventually, the music slows again. The screens rise

until there's only one left, hanging directly above the piano. The song grows simpler, quieter, as it switches back to Dorothy's famous solo. The last screen fills with a shot of our entire class, which I took last night during the dress rehearsal's curtain call. And I twirl toward the back of the stage and stand in the shadows as a field of real sunflowers grows slowly from the front of the stage.

(Okay, it's not really a field. It's more like a single row—but it spans the entire stage and looks as good as the real thing.)

The music trails off. The last screen fades to black and lifts. The regular stage lights come on.

And nothing happens.

I catch Megan's eye, then look out at the audience. They're not clapping or cheering. They're not running to their cars or throwing tomatoes at the stage either, but I expected more of a response than total silence.

"Bravo!"

I gasp.

In the front right corner of the auditorium, a man stands and claps with both hands overhead. Soon, a woman in the middle section joins him. Another woman joins her, and then another.

It doesn't happen right away, but it happens. We get a standing ovation.

"Ruby!" Megan shouts over the noise. She's still sitting on the piano bench, beaming.

I dash over to her, give her a big hug, and then look toward the lighting booth. I jump up and down and wave to Sam. I'm worried his shyness will keep him from accepting the recognition he deserves, but a few seconds later, I see him jogging down an auditorium aisle. When he reaches us, he hugs me before I can do the same to him.

"You were amazing," he says next to my ear.

Which just about makes me fall right off the stage.

We bow four times because people just keep clapping. On the first bow, I spot Ava, Stephanie, and Hilary standing with their families. They're not clapping, but they don't look like they plan to storm the stage and drag us off by our hair. On the second bow, I see Mr. Fox cheering and whistling. On the third bow, I see Miss

Anita talking with a man wearing a three-piece linen suit and scribbling in a fat notebook. She catches me looking at her, and she actually smiles. She pats the man's arm and motions to me. He smiles too, then makes a Y with one hand and mouths for me to call him.

Luis Lobo. The talent agent.

On the fourth bow, I spot Momma and Nana Dottie. They're both laughing and crying as they share a pack of tissues and blow me kisses. I see Oscar, too. He's standing next to Nana Dottie, and he winks and gives me a thumbs-up.

And then I spot one more person, and I almost fall off the stage a second time.

Gabby. She's standing next to Momma, grinning and taking my picture with the best present I've ever gotten.

Until now, anyway.

21.

"Did you go swimming? And walk on the beach? And hug a palm tree? And eat cheesy chicken burritos, just because you can?"

"Not today." I smile at the wistfulness in Gabby's voice. She and Momma had worked together to surprise me with a visit, and though she was here for only three days, just long enough to see Citrus Star and take a quick tour of Coconut Grove, that was all the time she needed to fall in love with the place. "But we'll definitely do all those things and more when you come back during Christmas break."

"I can't wait! I've been crossing off the days on the Miami calendar I bought at the airport." She pauses, and I hear her flipping through pages. "Which, by the way, could really use a few pictures taken by famed local photographer Ruby Lee."

"Speaking of pictures, did you get the ones I sent this morning?"

"Of your mom and grandma playing Twister?" She giggles. "Yes. Those positions did *not* look comfortable."

"Nana Dottie's tough. Momma spent the night with three ice packs and a heating pad."

Nana Dottie winks as she walks by with a picnic basket and folded blanket.

"Anyway, we're about to leave so I should get going." I stand up from the couch. "I just wanted to say hi on Momma's brand-new cell phone."

"Oh my goodness, if you'd told me three months ago that your mom would own a phone that wasn't attached to a wall, I would've asked if the moon was made of green cheese, too."

I watch Momma type something into the computer. "At this rate, it probably is."

We promise to e-mail with updates tomorrow and hang up.

"Sweetie, come look at this!"

I hurry across the living room and stand behind Momma. She and Oscar are sitting at the desk with my laptop open in front of them. "Is that you?" I ask, peering over her shoulder.

"Can you believe it?" She shakes her head and laughs. "I'm *on* the *Internet*. For the whole world to see. Right this minute, someone in Paris or London or Tokyo might be looking at me. *Me*. Little Francine Lee!"

"If they're not right this minute, they will be soon," Oscar says. "It won't take long for Purls of the Grove to become an international sensation."

Momma looks at him. "I've only gotten ten orders."

"From one store," Oscar says pointedly.

"That wants to sell each tote bag for three hundred dollars," I remind her. "And that's already sold six of the ten based on the display sample you sent."

She shrugs and looks at the screen again. "Who knew that when EcoChic turned me down for a job, they'd eventually give me a new career? Doing what I love to do more than anything—besides hanging out with my favorite girl, of course."

"Everything happens for a reason," I say. This is another of her favorite mottos and has never seemed truer. Only a few weeks after being turned down by EcoChic, Momma got a call from Clementine, the store's owner. Apparently, Clementine loved the white knitted tote bag Momma carried that day so much, she wanted to sell it—and others like it—in her store. That vote of confidence was just what Momma needed, and it even inspired her to start her own business.

"So the website's done for now." Oscar clicks the mouse to show each feature. "People can browse products, place orders, and contact you directly via an online form. When you're ready, I'll show you how to update it yourself."

"And you'll also show me everything else, right?

The spreadsheets and accounting and numbers stuff?"
Momma sounds excited but nervous. This is completely understandable, considering that she lost her job at Nana Dottie's country club because she didn't know her way around the computer.

"Absolutely." Oscar releases the mouse to squeeze her hand.

"And I can teach you e-mail," I offer. "I've gotten pretty good at it. I can even send attachments."

"You've both come a very long way."

We turn to see Nana Dottie standing in the living room doorway, car keys in hand.

"And I couldn't be prouder," she continues. "But it's time to go. You know I hate to be late."

Nana Dottie's definitely mellowed in recent weeks, but there are a few issues she still takes very seriously. Punctuality is one of them. Normally, her announcement of hating to be late would make Momma check her watch and pretend to be panicked, which would make me try not to laugh. But I'm not laughing now. I don't want to be late to where we're going either.

I grab my backpack from the couch and hurry after Nana Dottie. Momma and Oscar follow behind me, talking about websites, spreadsheets, and how he'll give her a thorough lesson after their dinner date tomorrow night. I'm tempted to turn around and take their picture, but I'm more reluctant to slow down. Plus, something tells me there will be many more photo opportunities with those two.

"Do you want me to drive, Mom?" Momma asks when we reach the garage. Nana Dottie's mellowed so much she's been letting Momma use the Jaguar until Momma saves enough to buy us a new car.

"I thought we'd take the convertible," Nana Dottie says, already popping the trunk.

Momma and I exchange surprised looks. The convertible's been locked in the garage since it left the shop with a new front bumper two weeks ago. Nana Dottie seemed pretty upset that the car was no longer exactly the same as it was when Papa Harry last used it, so we assumed it'd be a long, long time before she drove it again. *If* she drove it again.

"Shotgun!" Momma declares suddenly.

"The last time she said that we ended up in a ditch," I warn Oscar as Momma runs to the convertible.

"All in the past, Ruby Lee! And the past is a long time ago."

I think about this as we get in the car and start driving. The past *does* seem like a long time ago. It's hard to believe that it's only been three months since we packed up everything we owned, said good-bye to our family and friends, and left the only home we'd ever known. It feels like entire years have passed since we pulled up to Nana Dottie's house for the first time, signed me up for school, and went computer shopping. Even everything that happened once I started school—circling the cafeteria at lunch, being teased by Ava Grand, hiding my lunch box, doing whatever I could to fit in—seems like it was an eternity ago. Some of the details have even grown fuzzy, just like they do as more and more time goes by.

Thank goodness I took so many pictures along the way. None of it was easy, but it also got us to this point. For that, I'll always want to remember.

"Is that rain?" Momma shoots up in the passenger seat and inspects a smattering of droplets on the windshield. "Do you think it'll be canceled?"

"It's just a little shower," Oscar says. "I bet it clears up before we get there."

He's right. By the time we pull into Coconut Grove Square five minutes later, the rain has lightened to mist.

"Aren't you going to put the top down?" Momma asks Nana Dottie once we've parked.

"It's still damp, Francine."

"Yes . . . but it's a drive-in. How will Ruby and Oscar see the screen?"

"We'll just roll down our windows and stick our heads out." I demonstrate. It's not ideal, but it does the job.

"This is ridiculous," a familiar voice says.

I pull my head in when Ava Grand stomps by. Stephanie and Hilary hurry to keep up. They're wearing their usual uniform of pastel sundresses and shiny metallic sandals. Seeing them makes me think of my gold sandals, which I haven't worn since the day I found out Miss Anita had made me the lead in Constellation. It's not that I don't like them or even that they bring back bad memories . . . it's just that my red Converse are so much more comfortable.

"I mean, a *drive-in*?" Ava huffs. "With a black-and-white movie? What kind of small-town, old-fashioned, boring hick event is this? Who planned it? Why are we here?"

"I actually think it might be fun," I hear Stephanie whisper to Hilary as they pass our car.

"You'd think she'd be happier after winning Citrus Star," Momma says, noticing them. "Isn't that what she wanted?"

"I guess it wasn't enough," I say. "She's still mad that Constellation didn't close the show. And she's *really* mad that Luis Lobo is interested in working with Sam, Megan, and me, even though we came in second place."

"I'm still amazed that you pulled that off in such a short time," Nana Dottie says.

"Me too. But it's a good thing we landed in that ditch. Opening my eyes to all the pictures I'd been taking and had just developed gave me the initial idea, and then Megan and Sam worked really, really hard to make it happen."

"Well, it sounds like a small-town, old-fashioned, boring hick event is exactly what Miss Sore Winner needs," Oscar says. "Maybe it'll help bring her back down to earth. Popcorn, anyone?"

"Extra butter, please!" Momma calls after him as he slides out of the car and starts toward the snack stand.

"A drive-in *does* seem more Curly Creek than Coconut Grove," I say, resting my chin on the top of the front seat.

"And what are the chances that they'd show *this* movie of all movies?" Momma turns slightly to kiss my cheek.

Nana Dottie brushes an imaginary speck of dirt from the dashboard. "Sometimes it doesn't hurt to use your connections," she says casually.

My mouth falls open. "You did this?" I look around.

The park is packed. People are sitting in their cars, relaxing in lawn chairs near their cars, and lounging on picnic blankets in the grass. If not for the palm trees, the same scene could be found in Curly Creek.

"Momma," Momma says softly, which makes me smile. I've never heard her call Nana Dottie that before. "It was very nice of you to do this for us."

"I didn't do it just for you." She looks at me, then at Momma. "I did it for me, too."

"It's starting!" I squeal as the screen lights up. "I've seen *The Wizard of Oz* a million times, but never like this."

"Come up front," Momma says, patting the spot between her and Nana Dottie. "You need to get the full effect."

I scramble across the backseat and throw the door open.

"Ruby!"

I look up to see Megan waving from a nearby patch of grass. She's with her parents and two other girls I recognize from school.

"We have plenty of room!" she calls out. "Want to join?"

"Maybe after the movie?" I call back.

She gives me a quick thumbs-up and flops down on their blanket. I'm just about to open Momma's door when I feel a light tap on my shoulder.

"Hey, you."

"Sam." My smile grows as wide as the movie screen behind me. "Hi."

"Hey." He looks down at his sneakers, then back up at me. "You look nice."

Now *I* look down. I don't think I look any different than usual in my jeans, yellow South Beach shirt, and Converse . . . but if he thinks the combined effect works, I'm glad. "Thanks. So do you." It's true. I've been noticing more and more lately how cute Sam is. The fact that he's nice, smart, and talented only makes him even cuter. "Are you here with your parents?"

He nods. I think he's going to say something else, but instead he slides his hands into the pockets of his jeans and looks toward the snack stand.

"Well, it was good to see you," I finally say. "I guess I'll—"

"Do you want to hang out sometime?"

I raise my eyebrows. He's still looking at the snack stand, so I turn slightly to see if this invitation was meant for someone else.

"I like you."

I turn back. His eyes find mine, and I can see right away how nervous he is.

"You're different from anyone I've ever met. You make me laugh. You make me . . . not want to hide." This last admission causes him to look away again. "And I don't know, I just thought maybe, if you wanted to, we could sort of—"

"Yes." I duck my head until our eyes meet. "I'd love to."

He grins. "Really?"

"Absolutely. Anytime."

"Okay." He takes a deep breath. "Great. I'll call you later then."

"I expect details, missy," Momma says once Sam's

out of earshot and I turn back to the car. She's standing outside, holding open the door. "Though that smile certainly says a lot."

"Does it look familiar?" I tease. "You've been wearing one just like it a lot lately."

"In the car." Her face is pink as she glances at Oscar, who's loading up on popcorn and sodas.

I climb into the front seat. Momma climbs in after me and closes the door.

"This is the best." I sigh happily as the screen fills with the familiar gray cloud and the opening credits start.

"I need chocolate," Momma says.

"Goodness gracious, Francine." Nana Dottie shakes her head. "You had an enormous lunch. And Oscar's bringing you ten pounds of greasy popcorn. That's not enough?"

"It's the salty-sweet combo," I explain to Nana Dottie. I stand on my knees and reach for my bag in the backseat. "Fortunately, I came prepared."

"You *do* love me!" Momma gasps when I hand her a chocolate cookie.

"Nana Dottie and I made them this morning. They're low in sugar and fat, but you'd never know it."

Momma looks doubtful but eats the cookie anyway. Her eyes widen as she chews. "Need more."

I start to take a handful of cookies from my ABBA lunch box so that I can put it back in my bag, but then I change my mind. I leave the cookies where they are and carefully place the lunch box on the dashboard for easy access. It's the first time I've ever publicly displayed the Dancing Queen.

It won't be the last.

"Well, would you look at that," Nana Dottie says quietly a few seconds later. She's leaning against the driver's side door, her eyes raised toward the sky.

Momma and I lean forward and look up. There's nothing to see through the windshield but light blue sky.

"I've been afraid to put the top down." Nana Dottie sits back. "I worried about ruining the pristine interior . . . and I also worried it would hurt. I didn't think I could enjoy the ride without Harold here with me."

Momma gently takes my hand in hers.

"But you have to take the chance, right?" Nana Dottie gives Momma and me a small smile. "You have to try. It might hurt at first . . . but it also might end up feeling better than you ever thought it could."

"No pain, no gain," Momma says softly.

Nana Dottie looks at the button to the right of the steering wheel. Her hand trembles as she reaches forward. The tip of her pointer finger stops an inch before the button. I glance through the windshield to see Dorothy in the first of my two favorite scenes. She's in black and white, and so is everything and everyone around her.

And then I see red. And orange. And yellow, green, blue, and a sliver of purple. They appear one by one as the convertible top lowers.

It's a rainbow. Rising out of Coconut Grove and tilting north. It fades somewhere above us, but I think it keeps going, stretching across two thousand miles, all the way back to Curly Creek. Connecting my two homes like a long road I traveled in red Converse.

I also think I now have three favorite parts in *The Wizard of Oz.*

The beginning. The end. And all the colors in between.

DANI NOIR

*A story about big lies, mysterious secrets,
and a tween girl turned sleuth . . .*

NOW AVAILABLE

FROM ALADDIN
Published by Simon & Schuster

Do you love the color pink?
All things sparkly? Mani/pedis?

These books are for you!

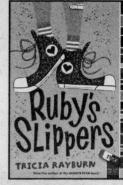

FIVE GIRLS. ONE ACADEMY. AND SOME SERIOUS ATTITUDE.

CANTERWOOD CREST

by Jessica Burkhart

TAKE THE REINS
BOOK 1

CHASING BLUE
BOOK 2

BEHIND THE BIT
BOOK 3

TRIPLE FAULT
BOOK 4

BEST ENEMIES
BOOK 5

LITTLE WHITE LIES
BOOK 6

RIVAL REVENGE
BOOK 7

HOME SWEET DRAMA
BOOK 8

CITY SECRETS
BOOK 9

Don't forget to check out the website for downloadables, quizzes, author vlogs, and more!

www.canterwoodcrest.com